DRAGON MOUNTAIN

By

Nancy Griffiths Beaman

ISBN: 0-75966-455-2

This book is printed on acid free paper.

1stBooks - rev. 10/25/01

To the children and teachers
who died in the school at Aberfan

CHAPTER 1

Coiled around the sleeping village of Pontnewydd, Dragon Mountain lay still. Its green slopes undulated above the river valley as they had from times long past. Its black head had been formed more recently from the coal dust and slag left behind after the good coal dug from deep underground had been brought to the surface and sent away by train and freighter to a world needing fuel.

The fiery fingers of dawn prodded the dragon into wakefulness and rays of red fire flashed through the darkness. Dragon Mountain stirred uneasily in the morning mist.

Hugh awoke, his heart pounding. He opened his eyes, his body still rigid with fear. He saw the familiar outline of the wardrobe and his trouser legs dangling from the hook on the half open door. He relaxed and closed his eyes. But the dream was still so strong he felt himself being dragged back into terror.

Gathering all his powers of resistance, he sprang from the warm bed into the cold, but safe atmosphere of the bedroom. He noted that his brother, Iestyn, was still asleep, his breath making visible puffs into the unheated air. Hugh grabbed his clothes and dressed quickly. He went along the narrow passage that led to his parents' bedroom and the small corner room where his sister slept.

Megan was sitting up in bed, braiding her long brown hair. Hugh could hear his mother moving around in the kitchen below, setting dishes on the table for breakfast. His father must have left already for the early shift at the mine, 6 a.m. to 2 p.m. He usually lit the fire before he left, and banked it up with small coal so that the house would be warm by the time the family got up for school. He must have overslept today. His mother must have just set a match to the paper and sticks under the coal in the fireplace. No heat came up the stairs.

Megan had most of her clothes on even though she was still in bed. Practical Megan, Hugh thought. She had taken her clothes from the chair next to her bed, and warmed them with her body before wriggling into them while still within the warmth of the blankets. Megan turned her head and saw him standing in the doorway.

"Pass me my dress, Hugh," she said, slipping her bare arms under the bedclothes while she waited for him to comply. Her red Sunday dress was hanging from the bureau near the window. Hugh wondered why his sister would wear it on a school day. Then he remembered. This was no ordinary day. It was March 1st. There would be no regular classes since it was the day when Welshmen everywhere celebrated St. David, the patron saint of Wales. They would sing the traditional songs and compete in the school eisteddfod for prizes in poetry, singing and elocution.

"Come on, Hugh. Hurry up. Throw my dress over."

Hugh moved quickly to the window, pausing to toss the dress on the way. He looked up at the inch of cold blue sky that was all that was visible above Dragon Mountain. It was so close that their vegetable garden was reclaimed from its pastured slopes, and they had to climb a steep flight of steps to get to it.

As Hugh looked at the mountain, his dream returned, and he shuddered, not just from the cold.

He turned back to his sister, away from the terror that still unnerved him, and climbed on the brass rail at the foot of her bed.

Not looking at her as he teetered along his make-believe tight rope he said, “Let’s skip school, today.”

“Mam would kill us,” said Megan, her head through her dress which sprayed around her pillows like a pool of blood. As she spoke she snuggled her arms back under the bedclothes.

“Not today, there’s no lessons. It’s St. David’s Day, as if you didn’t know. All we do is sing the old songs. Besides, we come home at lunch time.”

“Well, that’s all the more reason to go, silly! The sun’s out at last and we can play all afternoon.” Megan pushed her arms into her wool dress, and sprang fully dressed to the oval woollen rug beside her bed.

“You’ve even got your shoes and socks on!” cried Hugh.

“Don’t tell Mam about the shoes. I do wipe them off before I go to bed, which is more than *you* do. I hate to start the day with cold feet,” replied Megan. “I thought that rain would never stop. If I didn’t know that St. Swithin’s Day was in July I’d have thought we’d have had rain for forty days and nights.”

“Stop stalling,” said Hugh, falling off the bedrail into the rumpled blankets. Swinging his legs to the side of the bed, he glared at his sister. “Are you coming up the mountain with me, or not?”

Megan turned from the bureau mirror with a ribbon bow in her hand. “I know why you don’t want to go to school today.”

Hugh felt Megan’s eyes boring into him.

“You don’t think you can win the contest this year with that new boy from England having such a good voice and all.”

Hugh buried his face in the pillow and tried to do a headstand against the wall. He collapsed on the bed, and tried again. He held the position this time and came down slowly.

"Now, who's stalling?" said Megan.

"It's not that I care about losing. I'd like to win, of course. I've won three years in a row. But I'd hate to lose to *him*." It would be humiliating to lose to a stranger, not even Welsh, on that special day when all Wales celebrates its national saint.

Megan nodded. Her fingers stopped braiding the long strands of brown hair but still held them so that they wouldn't unwind. "All right, I'll go. Maybe Mam and Dad won't find out. But let's take Iestyn, too."

Hugh knew his parents would find out when they asked about the song contest that he wouldn't be entering, but he didn't want to say anything that would change Megan's mind. Taking Iestyn was another matter.

"He'll slow us down," he said.

Megan's jaw jutted, and Hugh knew he was in for an argument if he didn't agree. Besides, he was so glad that she was going to join him he would have agreed to almost anything. It would dilute their parents' wrath if they both went.

"Iestyn may not want to come. It's quite a pull up the mountain if you can't use your legs. 'Specially when the grass is wet." Hugh knew he would have to do most of the pulling of Iestyn's cart. He felt a little ashamed thinking that. Hugh remembered how sick Iestyn had been when he was four years old. They'd had to tiptoe around the house. Though Iestyn had recovered, he hadn't been able to use his legs ever since. His shoulders were powerful, though, and even though he was three years younger than Hugh, he could win at arm wrestling.

"Where're you going? I'll come too!" Iestyn clumped along the passage on his crutches. His red hair stood up in spikes above his pale face. His feet in thick wool socks trailed limply behind his sturdy pyjama-clad body.

"Sh, we don't want Mam to know," said Hugh, moving quickly to peer down the stairs anxiously. "Get dressed as fast as you can. We're going up the mountain."

As Iestyn's mouth formed a question, Megan put her hand over it and pointed him back to his bedroom. "We're cutting school today," she whispered soundlessly. "Explain later."

"Breakfast's ready," Peg Jenkins called. "And Welshcakes hot from the bakestone when you've finished your eggs."

After breakfast the three Jenkins children set off up the street as though going to school. "Come back, Hugh," his mother called. "Change into your Sunday trousers. You can't stand up in front of the whole school in those old trews!"

Hugh hesitated. Then, shrugging uncomfortably at Megan, he ran indoors to change.

The small procession set off again. Hugh pulled the handle of Iestyn's cart. Made from the old baby carriage all three of them had ridden as infants it sat lower to the ground and had a legless wooden chair nailed to its base. The wheels squeaked and the metal handle groaned as Iestyn bounced in his seat making automobile horn sounds. They looked back and waved at their mother who was still on the front step looking after them.

"I feel awful going up the mountain in our good clothes," said Megan.

"I feel bad too," said Hugh, "but Mam would have guessed.

We can always be careful." And he kicked at a stone, missed it and fell flat on his face.

"Sure," said Megan with a laugh, as she grabbed for the cart to stop it running over Hugh.

"Mam's gone in now," said Iestyn. "Up the mountain we go!"

CHAPTER 2

The morning air was clear and still. The treeless mountain slopes glistened after the spring rain. Suddenly, disturbing the silence, a few pieces of slag tumbled from the top of Dragon Mountain, scraping and jostling their way to the valley below. There was no-one close enough to wonder what had dislodged them from the pile.

Hugh had been right. It was hard work pulling Iestyn's cart up the rocky path. The wheels complained noisily. Megan started to push from behind. She's a pretty good sister, at that, he thought. Ahead of them, two mountain sheep, free to roam at will until shearing time, browsed the short grass. They were grey and dirty, their wool all matted from scrambling through barbed wire fences and over garden walls. Many's the time Hugh had chased them out of their vegetable garden.

"Let's stop for a rest," Hugh pulled a blade of grass through his teeth, making it squeak. It tasted bitter, he thought. He looked up as he stretched out on his back. White clouds, almost like sheep, nibbled at the blue sky. The grass felt damp but springy under him.

"Maybe we'll see some lambs," said Megan. "'See the head first, you'll be pushed ahead. See the side first you'll be pushed aside.'" she chanted. "'See the tail first you'll...' I forget what happens when you see the tail first."

Iastyn interrupted, "Isn't that Cyril Roberts behind that bush?"

"Oh, he's never very far from Megan," snickered Hugh. Megan sniffed in disdain. "I can't stand him. And he's always mitching. We look out the window at spelling class and he's out chasing butterflies or something."

"Maybe he thinks because you are mitching today that you are chasing him!" Hugh put his hands on his hips, stretched his neck, and squeaked, "I'm sooo pretty!"

Megan shrieked and came at him, fists flailing. She pushed him over and they rolled about until she sat on his chest. Hugh held her wrists so tightly that she finally shouted for a truce, and they lay panting until they'd caught their breath.

"We're almost at the Spout where we can get a drink," said Iestyn. "Come on, you two."

From a pipe that stuck out of the side of the mountain gushed the coldest, purest water. People from miles around brought jugs and bottles to be filled because it was more refreshing than the water in the taps outside their houses. When Hugh's parents married, Grampy had had the tap put inside the house as a wedding present. It was good not to have to go outside on a cold winter morning to fill the kettle for breakfast, but it was fun to lie on the cool, prickly grass and drink right from the spring at any time of the year, getting a clean face in the bargain.

"Wait till I fill my bottle," said Iestyn, as Hugh grabbed the handle of the cart when they'd all drunk their fill. "I'll probably be thirsty again by the time we reach the park."

Tennis courts, a bowling green, and free places to play and use play equipment had been set up on terraces close to the summit of the mountain. It was here the striking miners met to air their grievances and listen to speakers as they sat on the grass. Hugh hadn't understood too much of what was happening at the time. The General Strike had happened and the mines had been idle for a long time. No money came in and Mam had found weird and wonderful ways to feed them. Hugh remembered the Bovril and mashed potato sandwiches fried in bacon fat. He hadn't even missed the meat.

"Time for another rest," he said.

"We must have lost Cyril," said Iestyn. Sitting in his cart with his back to Hugh, he had the best view of the valley below. Hugh turned and looked down. The River Rhondda snaked its way through the naked hills, their trees long ago harvested for pit props. The floor of the valley was only wide enough for two streets and the railway line which ran alongside the river. All the other streets hung like ropes on the rounded mountain slopes. The slate roofs of the small stone houses glistened greyly in the morning sunshine. Church spires pointed warning fingers, making Hugh feel guilty. But only a little. He turned away from the sight of the school house, its roof grey like the others, and the muted sound of the school bell summoning all the children of Pontnewydd to come to school.

He could see the three buildings squatted in a network of yards—one playground each for the Infants' School, the Juniors, where Megan and Iestyn went, and the Seniors, where Hugh attended. Rimming the playgrounds were the foul-smelling outside toilets.

"Look," cried Iestyn, "a toy truck!"

"That's Tom Davies, the Milk. We'll miss snack time today," said Megan. "But I don't care!" She started skipping around Iestyn's cart, and he threw himself out and started rolling around.

Guilt gave way to a feeling of wild abandon. The mitching, thought Hugh, was an accomplished fact. It was too late to turn back. They might as well enjoy it and worry about the consequences later.

"Now, class, come to order," he said, a grin belying the sternness in his voice. "I am going to take attendance."

"Megan Jenkins!"

"Present," piped Megan.

"Iestyn Jenkins!"

"Present," answered Iestyn in a gruff voice.

"Cyril Roberts!"

"Absent," said Megan.

"No, I'm not. I'm present, too," said Cyril, coming out from his hiding place behind the shed where the tennis nets were stored.

"Oh, Cyril, the whipper-in is always looking for you," said Megan. "If he sees you with us he'll know for sure we're mitching too!"

"Let him come along," said Hugh. "We can't stop him anyway."

CHAPTER 3

Mr. Thomas scanned the empty desks. "Hugh Jenkins is rarely late. Is he sick? Does anyone know?" He looked up as the door opened. In scurried a latecomer, but it wasn't Hugh.

"I'll take attendance after devotions today. Maybe the tardy ones will be here by then."

The class quieted.

"Psalm 46," Mr. Thomas announced. "God is our refuge and strength, a very present help in trouble. Therefore will not we fear, though the earth be removed and the mountains be carried into the midst of the sea..."

Hugh breathed deeply. Their father always told them to do this when they climbed high above the smoke and coal dust.

"Breathe in," he'd say. "Now, out slowly..." Hugh quickly suppressed the thought of his father. "Come on, let's explore the monastery ruins."

They passed the huge boulder marked with an X etched into the stone where Prince Rhys had been beheaded in one of the skirmishes with the English invaders long years before. The mountain was called Penrhys after him. The head of Rhys. With a shudder Megan looked the other way.

"We don't know if it really happened," said Hugh, who usually knew what his sister was thinking. "There's no historical evidence he was killed right here."

Swinging through the tall iron gate through which only one person could pass at a time, Hugh felt the ground tremble.

"What's that?" asked Iestyn.

"Thunder, I think," said Cyril.

"More like an earthquake," ventured Megan.

"Look," shouted Hugh. "Look over there. The tip! It's moving!"

Hugh started to run back the way they had come. The iron gate screeched. He pointed at the man-made mountain of slag and waste coal that dominated not only the village but the green mountain slopes that had been there for centuries.

"Oh, Duw, it's sliding down to the school!"

"Stop taking the Lord's name in vain, Cyril Roberts," said Megan.

"It's an avalanche," cried Hugh.

The two weeks of heavy rain must have separated the grains of small coal which were bound together loosely by the short-rooted weeds and ferns that grew freely in and over them, greening its mass into an artifical mountain. The dragon-shaped head had disintegrated into a slow moving river of mud which oozed with gradually increasing speed into the valley below.

"The school!" screamed Megan. "It's going right for the school. The mud will cover it!"

"The school wall is high. Surely it will stop at the wall," said Hugh with what he hoped was a reassuring tone.

Iestyn held on to the sides of his cart until Hugh could see his fingers turn white.

On, on, went the slithering avalanche, filling the school yards, piling up against the grey stone walls, climbing up to the red brick window facings. With the sound of a hundred shotguns the windowpanes cracked. A high keening sound hurt their ears so that they covered them with their hands to keep out the sound.

Hugh grabbed Iestyn's shoulder so hard he cried out.

"The school! It's covered with mud from the tip!" Hugh shouted.

"Where are all the kids?" asked Cyril.

"They must have run out the other side," said Megan.

"Come on. Maybe we can help," cried Hugh, running back down the mountain.

"Wait for me!" shouted Iestyn, crawling out of his cart and struggling to pull himself erect on his crutches. He moved quite fast along the level path but when it dipped steeply downward he lost his balance and rolled until he caught up with his brother. Hugh stood hesitant, his first instinct to rush to the buried school stopped by his brother's predicament. He helped Iestyn up and propped him up against the high stone wall which served as a boundary fence for one of the mountain farms.

Megan had picked up Iestyn's crutches and Cyril was pulling the empty wagon. "Ouch," he yelled, as it overran him and banged into his heels.

Suddenly, Megan screamed. "Climb on the wall. It's coming this way!"

Hugh looked to the right, tearing his eyes away from the buried school with a conscious effort. What he saw made him forget the plight of the children in school. The avalanche had fanned out and was indeed coming their way. The slow black tide made a sickening scraping, gurgling sound as it dragged stones and bushes and whatever was in its path along with it. Like a reptilian monster it moved inexorably to swallow them up.

CHAPTER 4

Tom Davies, the Milk, piled the crates of empty bottles from yesterday's snack at school into the back of his truck. He looked back to check the number of full bottles he had just left on the front porch of the school. Yes, the number ordered. Gwilym Edwards and Dai Jones, monitors for the week, were just lifting two of the crates to take them to the classrooms. "Bore da, boys. Don't drop any today, eh?" The boys turned to wave, and the milkman gave his usual tongue-clicking signal to this horse.

A strange roar, unlike anything he'd ever heard before, caused him to drop the reins and turn around.

What he saw filled him with terror so that he couldn't speak. He waved his arms helplessly and pointed, his mouth open in a silent scream and his eyes wide and staring. The two boys started toward him, the better to see what caused his fright.

A huge wave was moving down the mountainside. Even as he watched, it poured over the wall and began to fill the school yard. "Boys, drop that milk and run to me as fast as you can." Not understanding his contradictory instructions, the boys stood still. They couldn't see the thick muddy tide that threatened to engulf them. So the milkman ran, and pushed the crates out of their hands, and rushed them to the van where the horse patiently waited for another signal to move on. Tom jerked the reins and clicked his tongue, and the horse, sensing the urgency of the moment, galloped out the school driveway, knowing where the next stop was out of habit.

His master was incapable of directing him. He was still watching the avalanche, It covered the whole school, even the school bell high above the steep-pitched slate roof. The bell clanged once as though calling for help. The sound stopped, abruptly silenced for ever, its clapper encased in black mud.

With a strange crunching sound as though an immense reptile were chewing its prey, bones and all, the school, its outbuildings, and playgrounds disappeared. The dragon of the mountain was perched upon it.

A small tide of milk flowed towards the milk lorry. "There'll be more than milk spilled here today," Tom thought. "On St. David's Day, too." And he whipped his horse on to spread the alarm.

Safe on the top of the wall, Hugh looked down. "Just like Pompei. We just studied about that in school."

"Except that was red hot lava from a volcano in Italy, and this is cold wet mud from a tip in Wales," said Megan.

Hugh rubbed his eyes as though to erase the sight. When he looked once more into the valley it was still there. But the school and the houses that adjoined it were gone. They were completely covered with mud. All that was visible was the school bell, its clapper silent as were the classrooms beneath it.

"It's coming closer!" Cyril's voice was shrill. The black mud licked the bottom of the wall, and the children screamed as they scrambled down the other side. Hugh felt the uncemented stones begin to move.

"Run to the left." Hugh scarcely recognized his own voice, so hoarse and strained it sounded.

Iestyn dropped his crutches and started crawling, dragging his useless legs behind him. Hugh ran back for the crutches.

Cyril stopped to help Megan when she stumbled. Megan grabbed the crutches when she saw Hugh and Cyril make a chair with their hands for Iestyn to sit in. They staggered on, stumbling, falling, crying, looking back at the pursuing monster. Hugh saw it was now frothing over the wall like a hugh wave breaking at the shore.

Suddenly, Hugh shouted, “The level. Let’s go inside!”

“We aren’t allowed. It’s dangerous.” Megan’s voice came in gasps.

Hugh’s face relaxed into a tremulous smile. “It’s more dangerous out here!”

During the General Strike the unemployed miners had dug tunnels into the mountainside to get coal, both to heat their homes and to sell for money to feed their families. This ‘level’ had been abandoned as too dangerous and had been boarded up. The boards were loose now as the Keep Out sign had often been ignored. Hugh pulled two loose ones apart, and as he held them, first Iestyn, then Cyril crawled through.

“You might have pulled some from the other end, Cyril,” snapped Hugh.

Iestyn was already grabbing and pushing from the inside for Megan to squeeze in. Hugh followed in the aperture he had made for the boys.

“Let’s pull them all down if we can,” he said. “We’ll need all the light and air we can get.”

Just as he finished speaking a slimy curtain of mud swished down over the entrance to the man-made cave.

“Sounds like Aunt Ciss’s bead curtain, doesn’t it?” said Iestyn.

“Wish it was, so we could run back and forth like we always do at her house,” said Megan.

Hugh put out his hand in the darkness. This curtain was thick and impenetrable.

"Is there another way out?" asked Cyril. "If not..." His voice died away.

No one answered. It was as dark as the blackest night now that the entrance was blocked. Hugh stretched out his hand and touched a rough sleeve.

"Who's that?" yelled Cyril.

"It's only me," said Hugh quietly. "It's so dark in here I just wanted to make sure I wasn't alone."

"Let's hold hands, just for a moment. I want to touch someone too." Megan giggled nervously. "Don't ever tell anyone what I just said. I'll never live it down."

"We may have to huddle together to keep warm," said Hugh.

"How long do you think we'll be here?" asked Iestyn. Hugh could hear a tremor in his little brother's voice.

"Well, the avalanche must stop some time. Then we can dig ourselves out. He remembered the school and shuddered. He hoped the kids had got out in time. Better not remind the others of that. We're just as trapped, he thought. "If only we had some light, we could at least see if there's another way out while we're waiting."

"Well, it so happens that I brought my torch. The one I got for my birthday," said Iestyn. "If it didn't get broken when I fell down."

Suddenly, a ray of light dispersed the darkness. They sat together in a small huddled group. A bit dirty, but otherwise all right. Behind them the solid black curtain. Ahead of them the tunnel went quite a distance before tapering off into a thin crack. Above their heads particles of coal embedded in the rock looked like fireflies in the waving shadows that moved to the unsteady light of the torch.

"Keep it still, Iestyn," said Megan sharply. "Let me hold it!"

"It's mine, I'm going to hold it," pouted Iestyn.

"No fighting, *when* we're going to get out of here it'll be because we stick together, and work as a team."

"Keep your old torch, Iestyn," said Megan. "But you'd better not waste it. Is it the same battery you got when the torch was new?"

"The same one you've been using to read under the sheet when Mam thinks you're sleeping?" asked Hugh, with a laugh. "Better turn it off. We'd better keep it for when we really need it."

The darkness hit like a blow, so that Hugh ducked his head. There was silence.

"It so happens that I have a box of matches," said Cyril. "Bad boy saves the day!" Hugh could imagine the smirk on Cyril's pudgy face.

"You still smoking, Cyril?" Megan's voice was disapproving. "You'll stunt your growth."

"You sound just like Mam, Megan," snapped Hugh. "Quit nagging Cyril. We'll be needing those matches when the torch gives out."

"What about gas?" asked Megan. "Will it be safe to light matches?"

"Good question, Meg." Hugh tried to think about what he'd learned about coal at school and from hearing the colliers talk.

The coal in this part of Wales was anthracite, hard coal. Bituminous coal, being more porous, formed methane gas when water seeped through it. With anthracite there was more danger from suffocation. When the oxygen was all used up they would not be able to breathe.

Hugh shuddered. Remembering the concern in Megan's voice, he said quickly, "We're too close to the surface for gas to form. Until a short time ago it was open to the air." He decided he wouldn't mention the other hazard. Time enough if it became necessary to lie close to the floor and stop talking to save their breath. Hugh pushed the unpleasant thoughts out of his mind.

"Shall I turn my torch on again," asked Iestyn.

"No, let's try a match. Do your stuff, Cyril. No, wait! Let's plan what we're going to do, first," cried Hugh.

"I vote we try to dig ourselves out the way we came in," said Megan. "But I don't even know which way that is!"

"It's like a scary game of Blindman's Buff when you can't even peep out of the sides of the scarf," said Iestyn.

"So that's what you do," said Hugh. "Next time we play I'll make sure you can't peep." If there is a next time, he thought. Then with cheerful positiveness, he went on, "If we're all agreed to dig out the entrance, we need your match now, Cyril, to sea where it is."

"Jawch, I've dropped the box!"

"Oh, Cyril!" Megan used the tone of exasperation she always used when talking to her classmate.

"Ouch, my head!" Now it was Cyril's turn to sound exasperated.

Hugh rubbed his head ruefully but said nothing.

"Everybody keep still and let me find them." Iestyn sounded amused.

"Hold off, they're my matches and I'll find 'em. Just don't nobody bump into me again!"

Hugh could hear Cyril scuffling around. "Don't step on them, Cyril," said Megan.

There was a scraping sound, once, twice, and then, "Three tries for a Welshman," shouted Cyril, and with a slight sputter the darkness was dispelled once more.

The children turned towards the blocked entrance. "Grab a board to use as a shovel," cried Hugh.

"Jawch!" yelled Cyril. And the light went out.

"Stop swearing," said Megan.

"You'd swear if you burned your finger," complained Cyril.

"Stick it in your mouth," said Megan. "Let's dig."

"How can I dig with a blister on my finger?" cried Cyril.

"We'll get worse than that before we're through," Hugh muttered. He guessed Megan heard him because she whispered an apology to Cyril and they moved to join Hugh and Iestyn who were already digging at the mouth of the tunnel.

The cave was silent except for the scraping sounds of digging and the occasional plop of a small stone falling to the floor of the tunnel.

"My stick keeps breaking." Megan ended the lull in conversation. "I'm going to use my hands. Ugh, it's cold, wet, and slimy."

"Pretend we're digging at the beach at Barry Island," said Iestyn. "The tide has just gone out and the sand is cold, wet, and slimy!"

"That's the idea, Iestyn," said Hugh. "Remember when we won the sand castle contest? What fun we had that day!"

"Yes," said Meg with a chuckle. "You put a crab in the moat and forgot, and it got your toe instead of mine!"

"Wet sand sticks better than dry for building anything at the beach," said Iestyn. "You'd better not drop anything in the dry sand. Remember when you dropped your sixpence that Dad gave you to go to the fair?"

"I found it though," said Megan.

"No, you didn't," said Hugh. "I saw Dad slip another one where you would find it."

"Did he?" asked Megan uncertainly.

"He did. He knew you'd still be mad at yourself for dropping the first one, so he arranged for you to find it again."

"He must be some man, your father," said Cyril. "Mine never even goes to the beach with me."

"I wonder if they'll have the donkeys there this year. It sure was fun when they had races."

"You stayed on better than anyone. You'd have won if your donkey hadn't stumbled close to the finish line."

"Wish we were at the end of this mud," sighed Hugh.

Sighs and grunts joined slaps and scrapes as the children with the renewed energy from their memories of happier days at the beach kept digging through the thick wall of gritty coal dust. Mixed with earth and stones and small branches it seemed welded together into an impenetrable barrier.

CHAPTER 5

Tom spread the news as he drove to the firehouse. Then, on his own initiative he went to the pit head and to Mr. Evans, the mine owner. "We need shovels and any other digging tools you've got," Tom shouted. And he explained what had happened to the school.

Mr. Evans turned white. "My children! The two of them are there!" He called out in a load voice, "Sound the alarm! Get all the men up from the mine!"

The foreman looked blank. The day shift was hard at work. "Hurry," yelled Mr. Evans. "All hands are needed at the school."

Luckily, the big earth-moving machine used to dig the foundation for the new dance hall was still in the village. "Get it over to the school," cried Mr. Johnson, the owner of the hotel and brewery. His son was going to sing that morning in the eisteddfod. "Take care how you dig!"

From the top of Dragon Mountain where farm laborers had been summoned to help, the school area looked like a giant ant hill. But the ants were people desperately digging to find their children under the damp heavy crust that imprisoned them.

"Has anyone made a hole to the outside yet?" said Hugh, stopping to flex his stiff fingers.

"It keeps filling in," said Cyril.

"Maybe we should dig from the top," said Megan. "How high is the opening anyway?"

"I could sit on someone's shoulders," said Iestyn.

"What's that noise?" asked Megan. "We've all stopped digging." Hugh listened. Abruptly the sounds stopped.

"It's not us," said Iestyn. "It sounds like someone hitting the wall with a pick-axe. Maybe someone knows we're here and is coming to get us."

"Let's pretend to dig, and really listen this time," said Hugh.

Half heartedly the four children continued their ineffectual scraping. "Listen," whispered Cyril. When they stopped, the sounds stopped.

"Maybe it's the knockers!" said Cyril, in a low, frightened voice.

"Don't be foolish," said Hugh quickly. "Who believes in the coblynau, the Knockers, these days?"

"Whaaat are they?" Iestyn's voice trembled.

"Well," said Hugh. "They're the wee folk, like the tylwyth teg, but these are supposed to live underground. They help the miners find coal. They're not wicked or anything like that. They help people."

"What do they look like?" asked Iestyn.

"I've never seen one, and I never dreamed they actually exist. They're like us only much smaller, about up to your waist, Iestyn." Megan's voice shook just a little.

Just then the sounds echoed again through the dark tunnel.

The blackness seemed heavy and Hugh felt he couldn't breathe. Were the sounds coming closer? Where could they run?

"At least they can't see us in the dark," said Cyril.

"They can if they're magic," said Iestyn.

Hugh moved closer to the mud barrier that blocked their escape. Panic swept over him and he could feel the press of other bodies scrabbling with him at the unyielding mud.

"Stop!" Hugh knew he had to get control of himself. "We must face this danger calmly, if there really is danger. We don't really know yet, do we?" The others stopped digging and waited for Hugh to continue. What could he say or do when his heart was racing with fear? Yet, he was the oldest. They all depended on him. "Let's have some light, Iestyn," he said quietly. Taking a deep breath, Hugh looked down the tunnel as the torch beam pierced the darkness.

"There's nothing there," he said with relief.

"If they're there, they're behind that rock fall," said Cyril.

"You did say they help people, didn't you?" Iestyn crawled a few feet forward. "Please, if you are the Knockers, please help us get out of this place." Megan moved towards her younger brother and he hid his face in her shoulder.

"Look!" Cyril's voice trembled. Around the fallen rocks came two small figures. Wearing miners' hats and carrying miniature pickaxes, aprons over their coal encrusted clothes, two little men, about two and a half feet tall, beckoned them to come.

Their faces, black with coal dust as were those of the miners coming home from the mines, smiled in friendly fashion, and then, with an air of solemnity, they beckoned to the children to follow them. When they stood still as far away as they could from the coblynau, the little men waved their arms, jumped up and down and then pointed, their lips moving in a language the children couldn't understand. Once more, they raised their pickaxes and pointed, and then disappeared behind the rocks.

"There's nothing for it but to follow them," said Hugh. "Let's get in line. I'll go first, then Meg, then Iestyn, and Cyril last." "I don't want to be last. I want to be in the middle," whined Cyril.

"I'll be last," said Megan, impatiently. "Change places but let's get a move on."

"Put out your torch, Iestyn, and Cyril can light a match." Hugh moved towards the place where they had seen the coblynau. "Hurry up, Cyril, I want to see where I'm going and the torch is getting faint."

Suddenly, there was a loud cracking sound. "Hurry," yelled Megan, "the ceiling's..." Her voice switched off just as the light went.

"Quick, light! I think Megan's buried!" Hugh shouted. "The weight of the mud has made the overhang fall in!"

CHAPTER 6

Three children had been found in the schoolyard on the side away from the mountain. They had been the lucky ones excused to go to the outside toilets. Quickly they were hugged and comforted and rushed to the St. John's ambulance team to have their minor cuts and bruises treated. Flying stones from the collapsing walls of the school were still hurtling across the playground. "Thank God!" shouted one woman who grabbed her little boy and held him so tight he was more frightened by his mother's fierce hugging than the run from the sliding mud.

Peg Jenkins hadn't stopped to take her apron off. She was digging with her hands and calling her children's names, hoping she would hear an answering cry that would tell her where to dig. "Here, Peg, take this shovel," said one of the firemen. "My children are all grown and away from the valley, thank the Good Lord."

They kept on digging in silence. What was there to say? Then, Ivor Jones stopped to rest, pushing his tall fireman's helmet back from his forehead and wiping the sweat from it. "If the classroom walls held, there'd be enough fresh air trapped in there to keep them alive for quite a while," he said. Peg nodded but did not stop digging. "I'm praying with my hands," she said. Then she looked up and saw her husband. She ran to him, and it was then, and only then, that she wept.

Silent women with tear-stained cheeks carried cups of hot tea to the diggers. The village of Pontnewydd had always been a friendly place but never before had they all worked together as they did now. The children belonged to all of them. The village worked to save its own.

Two children were found in a classroom closet. The rescuers reached them before the good air had been used up. Another boy was found unconscious, but still alive, under a teacher's desk. Mr. Thomas, the teacher of Standard 6, was carried out on a stretcher. They had found him with a girl under each arm, and a boy sheltering beneath his arched body. All were badly hurt, but still breathing.

"Ask him if he knows anything about Hugh," called Ted Jenkins.

"Later," said Dr. Orr, the red-haired Irishman who had been digging with every one else until the first casualties were found. "He can't talk now."

These rescues made everyone dig with renewed vigor. As hours passed they knew it was hopeless. There could be no one left alive under the heavy mound of mud. But they kept on digging. They had to find their loved ones. They had to know for sure what had happened to them. Even if it would be the last time they would see them, they had to see them once more.

Only Megan's patent leather shoes were visible sticking out from the pile of brown earth, mixed with black mud, that had fallen from the top of the tunnel entrance. The three boys fell upon the mound, digging with their hands to find Megan. Hugh estimated where her head would be, hurling clods of earth without caring where they fell. Patches of her red dress appeared and soon Hugh gently lifted her head and brushed earth from around her eyes and nose. "Oh, Meg, do wake up," he sobbed.

"Her nose is all clogged up," cried Iestyn. "Maybe she can't breathe."

He pulled a paint stained handkerchief from his pocket and cleaned the dirt from her nostrils. "Is paint poisonous?" he asked.

"Not the kind we use in school," said Cyril.

The three boys hovered over Megan's still form. Hugh rubbed her hands and then felt her pulse. "She's still alive. Do wake up, Meg!"

Megan stirred, and opened her eyes. "Well, I certainly copped it that time," she said, gently feeling the top of her head. She winced and lay down again, her head on Hugh's lap. "What's this, am I bleeding?"

"No," said Iestyn with a laugh. "I used a lot of red, painting The Welsh Dragon for St. David's Day."

"If we hadn't changed places I'd have been the one to get hurt," said Cyril. "Sorry I'm not sorry. But how was I to know the roof was going to fall in?" Hugh felt Megan bridle, even though her face was in shadow. Before she could make an angry retort, he said, "Well, *I'm* sorry. I wouldn't want any of us to get a shock like that."

"Thanks for digging me out so fast," said Megan. "There's a big bump on my head, but it could be worse. Help me up, Hugh."

"Don't move, Megan. I'm not exactly anxious to meet the Knockers around the next bend!" Cyril's fear matched Hugh's. But the danger from another ceiling collapse frightened him even more.

"Say," said Iestyn," you said the Knockers help people. Maybe they knew the ceiling was going to fall in. That's why they were calling us."

Hugh had noticed before how Iestyn often said something that answered what he was thinking. Good old Iestyn, he was braver than the rest of them put together!

"You could be right. They seemed harmless enough," said Hugh. "Let's get back in line and find out just what is around the bend, as Cyril said."

Step by step the procession moved slowly deeper into the tunnel. Hugh could hear Iestyn's crutches scraping and slipping on the stones at their feet. They were in total darkness again to conserve both battery and matches. "We'll have light when we look beyond the rocks that seem to be blocking the tunnel."

"Ouch!" Cyril recoiled from hitting his head on a projecting rock. "Keep behind me," said Hugh. "I have my hands out in front so we won't bump."

"We're at the rocks," said Hugh. "Now we need light."

Cyril pushed past Iestyn. "I'll strike one of my matches."

"Oh, no, you won't. I'm going to use my torch," cried Iestyn.

Hugh could feel draught and movement as the two boys struggled. "Hold it!" he yelled. "Just think. We must keep our heads and be practical. Cyril, if you strike a match, you'll burn your face or clothes looking past it. Now Iestyn's the smallest. He'll have less trouble than the rest of us squeezing through. Let him use the torch and if it looks safe he can go first."

"I know," said Cyril. "I'll hold the torch while he's going through."

"It's *my* torch, and I'm not going to give it to *nobody*," cried Iestyn.

"Baby," shouted Cyril. "Your name should be No-styn, not Yes-tyn!"

"Stop it, both of you. I've got a bad enough headache from my bump so cut out the yelling."

"Right. We've got to be a team," said Hugh. "Now, I know we're all sick of being shut in here in the dark and all. It's scary and its dangerous. But if we quarrel we won't stand a chance of getting out of here." Hugh felt his voice start to shake and controlled it with a conscious effort. "Now, who wants to be the leader?" he continued. "We should choose one person to decide what we do. Of course we can all give ideas. But if we all want our own way, it'll be a mess."

"Hugh's the oldest," said Megan. "I vote for him."

"Me, too," said Iestyn.

"Well, Cyril, do you want to be the leader?" Hugh hoped Megan wouldn't say anything to get Cyril's back up. Besides he really didn't care if he wasn't the leader.

"All right, Hugh. You be the leader," said Cyril. "But..." Cyril sounded reluctant.

"Of course, I'll need plenty of help from all of you," said Hugh quickly. "Now, Cyril, give me your opinion. Is the crack big enough for us to squeeze through?"

"I guess Iestyn will make it, easy. If he's going to go first and scout, the rest of us can take our chances," Cyril sounded mollified by Hugh's requesting his opinion.

"What if the Knockers are waiting for me?" asked Iestyn, uneasily.

"Shine the torch first," said Megan. "Remember, you were the one who asked them to help. And I think they did, but we were too slow and I got hurt."

"We can all look at the same time if some of you scrunch down," said Hugh. "Shine on, Iestyn."

“I’ll lie on the bottom. But don’t step on me!” said Megan. The boys pressed their faces to the crack.

“There’s no-one there” said Hugh, with great relief. “Do you want me to go first, Iestyn?”

“That’s all right, Hugh. If anything comes at me I can hit out with my crutch. Just don’t leave me out there too long,” said Iestyn.

Beyond the rocky barrier which Hugh assumed was an old rock fall the tunnel was almost as high as the one they were in. Iestyn shone the torch ahead and they could see that it went a distance into the mountain. No ray of daylight broke the blackness ahead of them. Hugh had hoped to see a way out, but could see none from his vantage point.

“Well, let’s join Iestyn. We may have to budge these rocks. It looks a tight squeeze,” said Hugh.

The rocks were too heavy to move but Megan managed, by scrunching her body into its smallest position and curving it around the aperture to join Iestyn. The torch light wavered, and Hugh saw Iestyn hold on to his sister as his crutches clattered to the ground. Brave little guy, thought Hugh. I shouldn’t have let him go first!

“Now, you, Cyril,” he said.

Cyril elected to make himself as tall and thin as he could. Then he found he couldn’t get his head through. “I’m stuck,” he whimpered. “Help me, I’m stuck!”

“Keep calm,” said Megan, with an unusual show of patience, for even Hugh was beginning to feel irritation at Cyril’s constant whining. “Get your legs and feet through first, and Iestyn and I will hold them so they don’t slip and make you bang your head,” she continued.

“My back hurts. I’m all twisted,” cried Cyril.

"Now, try moving your head slowly with your chin on your chest," she suggested. "Try to relax. You're too stiff."

Hugh watched Cyril's progress with trepidation. He was taller than Cyril, but thinner. He decided he'd try to get his head through first, and trust he could squirm his body after it.

"I think there's blood running down my face," moaned Cyril.

Iestyn shone the torch directly on Cyril. "No, it's sweat. But you are a bit scratched and red."

With a grunt and a groan Cyril collapsed on Megan and Iestyn. The torch went out as Iestyn crawled out from under Cyril.

Megan sighed. "It's so dark!"

Hugh said, "Let it stay that way. Maybe I'll do much better if I can't see the sharp rocks. I have a pretty good idea of the shape of the opening. I'll let my body find its own way through. If I need light I'll ask for it."

Hugh got his head through the widest part of the aperture with some skin scraping and scratching. He stopped and considered. He knew he could never get his head back through the hole so he *must* squeeze his body after it. He was *glad* nobody could see his predicament. It's like being in the stocks, he thought. A wild desire to laugh surged through him. Suppressing it he pulled in his abdominal muscles and, turning sideways pressed his torso into the irregularly shaped opening. For one tense moment he thought he was stuck. He felt his body flow slowly and then with a rush he fell down on the other side. Iestyn turned the torch on and they all hugged each other.

"We'll never get back that way," said Cyril lugubriously. "Hope there's another way out."

"Oh, Cyril," said Megan, with a laugh. "There is. There just has to be!"

CHAPTER 7

The night sky slowly darkened. It soon blended with the blackness that covered the school. There was no moon, but the grim scene was lit by floodlights from the mines, searchlights from the firehouse, and individually held miners' lamps wavering like fireflies.

The digging continued. No-one wanted to stop. The earth-moving machine had been pulled to the side and loomed like a prehistoric monster over the flattened mud pile.

"Look up at that seam of coal," said Hugh, and Iestyn directed the torch light above their heads. "Dad says a good collier would know just where to hit that seam so that it would separate from the rock as clean as a whistle."

One jab from a practised hand holding a pick, and the good coal would come tumbling down. Then the miners would load it by hand on the trams which would rattle it along the rails through a maze of tunnels to the cage. Then up the full tram would go to the mine head. There it would be hoisted aloft on the metal pulley which would swing it down to the unloading platform where it would be sorted and screened, again by hand. The different sized pieces would be sent various places. The railway cars stood waiting to take the coal to Cardiff, the largest port, where freighters waited to take it all over the world. Yes, Welsh coal was in demand all over the world, thought Hugh with pride.

"I wonder why they stopped mining here with such a good seam close at hand," said Megan.

"Looks easy to get at right here," echoed Iestyn.

"Hope it doesn't fall down on us," said Cyril.

"The Knockers were right when they banged here," said Iestyn. They all looked around uneasily. "They knew what they were doing all right. How could they know we aren't looking for coal. Just a way out."

"Where did they go?" asked Megan. "Maybe they'll come back if we call."

"No, don't," said Cyril.

Hugh felt the way Cyril must feel. He wondered if he had dreamed about the little men. No, the others saw them too. They'd find their own way out! "Let's go."

Leaning on his crutches Iestyn led the way. Since he couldn't hold the torch and crutches too he stuck it in his pocket.

"The battery's getting weak," he said. "I'll hold a crutch ahead of me once in a while."

"I think we'd better have some light. I keep treading on someone's heels," said Hugh. "Cyril, light up."

Suddenly, Iestyn yelled, "I'm falling..." His voice was cut off in a scream. Hugh jumped forward, and tripped over one of Iestyn's crutches. He heard a loud splashing sound and feared what he would see when Cyril's match dispelled some of the darkness.

Iestyn was dangling over the edge of a deep hole.

"Quick, grab his arms before he lets go." Hugh lay on his stomach and seized the back of Iestyn's jacket as Cyril grabbed his arms. The match went out, and the three held on to Iestyn, whose body swayed precariously over the abyss. Panting and grunting they hauled him up.

"Boy, you're heavy," grumbled Cyril.

"Light, Cyril," snapped Megan. By the small flickering flame, Hugh could see that Iestyn was all right. He lay inert and silent, his eyes reflecting the horror of his suspension over what seemed to be a bottomless pit.

"My crutch fell," he said tremulously.

Hugh, Megan and Cyril moved carefully to the edge and looked down. "There it is. It's floating. There's water down there." Megan pointed excitedly to what might have been a toothpick a giant had used and discarded. "Oh, it looks so small!"

"It's a long way down," said Hugh, thoughtfully. "Doesn't look too hopeful a way of escape."

"What's that light down there?" asked Cyril.

"You're holding it, silly," said Megan with a laugh, "It's a reflection."

Hugh turned back to Iestyn who was sitting up, and rubbing the strained wrists and fingers that had kept him from joining his crutch down below.

"Ow," cried Cyril as the match burned itself out on his finger and thumb.

Iestyn got out his torch and by the weakening beam of light Hugh could see that what he'd thought was a hole was encased in a circular wall. It had been broken through where they were, possibly by the striking miners who had dug the level in search of coal. Above them the wall rose sheer and straight ending in a small circle of light.

"That's daylight," shouted Hugh excitedly. "That's our way out!"

No one spoke as they looked at the slippery, almost perpendicular walls. Hugh contemplated climbing them and shuddered.

"Could this be a well?" asked Megan.

"Of course. It must be St. Mary's," said Hugh. "If so, we know where we are."

"Except we're a long way down," muttered Cyril.

Ffynnon Fair, or in English, Mary's Well, had become a shrine to the Mother of Christ. A statue of Mary and the Holy Babe had appeared miraculously in a large oak tree close to the spring which had been in existence on Penrhys Mountain since pagan times. No-one could remove the statue from the tree. One historical source stated that "the country folks believed that eight oxen could not have drawn the image of Penrhys from its place in the tree." Pilgrims came from miles around, and eventually a small stone chapel was erected over the well.

Then, and only then, so the story went, could the statue be removed from the tree and set within the chapel. The waters of the well become renowned for their healing powers, and pilgrims came to be cured of their ailments, both physical and spiritual. The Cistercian monastery, a humble offshoot of the abbey of Llantarnam in Monmouthshire, had been built on the top of Penrhys Mountain where the monks tended their sheep and worshipped God in the bleak solitariness of the Welsh hills. To these pastoral duties was added the responsibility of caring for these travelers.

Hugh remembered Mr. Thomas reading a poem written by a bard of the early 16th Century, Rhisiart ap Rhys. He couldn't remember it all though the teacher had asked them to memorize it.

> "Any disease, which seeks it there is healed—
> White wine runs in the streamlet,
> That can quell pains and fatigue.
>
> The diseases of the multitude
> Who call upon thee, after their weeping
> Are healed upon the second night."

When King Henry VIII had taken over the monasteries, the shrine over St. Mary's Well had fallen into disuse. Weeds and brambles climbed over the path, and children reverted to the old pagan customs by throwing a pin into the well for good luck. All that remained of the monastery was a broken down wall.

Megan interrupted Hugh's reverie with a practical question. "How are we going to climb up those steep walls?"

Iestyn, who seemed fully recovered from his terrifying fall, sang, "Oh, for the wings, for the wings of a dove...", the song Hugh often sang at eisteddfods, and they all laughed.

They peered upward. There was no light to cheer them.

"I wonder what the time is," said Hugh. "Daylight must have gone."

"Maybe we'd better wait till morning," said Cyril.

"What? Spend the night here? It's so cold and dark," cried Megan.

"Good thinking, Cyril," said Hugh. "At least we can see the top of the well when morning comes. We can huddle together to keep warm." Hugh yawned. "Now that we've stopped I do feel sleepy." He curled up and tried to get comfortable.

"I think Iestyn's asleep already," said Megan.

"No, I'm not. I'm too hungry to sleep. All I've got is a candy bar. I'll share it with you if you like."

"Hey, I've got some Welshcakes I put in my pocket when I went back to change into my trousers," said Hugh.

"And I've got an apple," said Megan. "I've been too scared to think of food, but now I'm starving!"

"Do you want a bite, Cyril?"

"No thanks," said Cyril curtly.

"Oh, come on, take a Welshcake," said Hugh, passing it over in the dark.

"What's that rustling noise?" said Iestyn.

The sound stopped abruptly. "I never go anywhere without plenty to eat," said Cyril. "And if you think I'm going to share it with you lot, you've got another think coming!"

"You're a pig, Cyril Roberts!" said Megan. "We don't want your mouldy old food!"

"Chew slowly, and make every bite last a long time," advised Hugh. "Let's save the apple for later, and, if you can stand it, Iestyn, the candy bar, too."

"Yes, we'll be even hungrier in the morning," said Megan.

The sound of Cyril's chewing seemed to grow louder after the Welshcakes had gone.

"Well, I'm going to try for a bit of shut-eye," said Hugh, yawning audibly. "How about you, Cyril?"

The chewing sounds stopped. "I dunno," said Cyril. Then after a pause, "I don't feel very hungry now. Take these two sandwiches and keep them for later. I'm so used to eating a lot they'll soon be gone. And here's a half sandwich for now. You didn't have much to eat. Keep the Welshcake for later too." And Hugh heard him squirming into a position for sleep.

Then Cyril's voice broke the silence. "I'm sorry I was greedy. No wonder you don't like me. Nobody likes me!"

"Don't be silly, Cyril," 'course we do," said Megan generously, and Hugh smiled in the darkness. Good old Meg!

"Yes," he said. "We're in this together. We're the four Welsh musketeers."

"Can this musketeer have a bite of that sandwich?" said Iestyn sleepily.

"You must fight for it. Get out your sword, sir! *En garde!*" shouted Hugh, and poked where he thought Iestyn's tummy would be. They rolled over, wrestling and pummeling until they were both out of breath.

"Don't squash the sandwiches we're saving for tomorrow, and keep away from the edge," shrieked Megan.

"Thanks, Cyril, I'm enjoying my bite of sandwich. Egg, isn't it? Mmmmmm..." And Iestyn snuggled down next to Hugh. "That warmed me up," panted Hugh. "If we lie close together we'll keep warm."

CHAPTER 8

When the new day stretched bloodstained fingers across the dark sky, Ted Jenkins led his wife home. They sat at the wooden kitchen table around which they had enjoyed so many family meals. There were crumbs of dried dough still clinging to its surface and a pile of cold Welshcakes on a plate. Peg had left everything when the mine whistle blew, thinking Ted had been the one in danger. Now here they sat, their three children gone, buried under the avalanche. She put her head on the table and sobbed. The first rays of the morning sun shone on her dark brown hair, so like Megan's that Ted could not keep the tears from his own eyes. He put his arm around his wife. He tried to find words to comfort her but there were none.

"Mrs. Jones said that God wanted all our children with Him in heaven. Well, I want my children alive and here with me!"

"I don't believe God would do anything so cruel," said Ted. "He's a God of love. Don't you think it's all a terrible accident, and not God's doing at all?" It was men who piled up all that slag and small coal, he thought. "Instead of carting it all away, they did the easiest thing because it didn't cost them anything." Ted's voice got louder and angrier. "Why didn't they find ways to bind the stuff together so a few days' rain wouldn't set it sliding on our village. It's greed and selfishness that caused it, not God!"

Now it was Peg's turn to comfort. "Let us ask God to help us bear this terrible happening." They sat in silence. "I will lift up my eyes to the hills, whence cometh my help. My help cometh from the Lord who made heaven and earth..." Peg wept as she remembered that Megan had read that psalm at Sunday School, just a few days ago.

"Meg, are you asleep?"

"No, Hugh, I can't get comfortable. Oh, for my soft feather bed instead of sharp stones digging into me!"

"I think Cyril and Iestyn are sleeping."

"Wouldn't you know that poor Cyril snores?" Megan laughed quietly.

"Remember this morning when you said you knew why I wanted to skip school? You were wrong. It wasn't because of the song contest." Hugh sensed that his sister sat up. If only he could see her. It was strange talking through a darkness so thick it was like being wrapped in a blanket. And a cold one at that! Could he really tell her the truth?

"Well, I had this dream, see. Promise you won't laugh?"

"I probably won't laugh at anything again until I'm out of this place," said Megan. Hugh knew her so well he could see her face, her jaw sticking out and her eyes flashing. Pity any tylwyth teg who tried to push her around!

"Oh, Meg," he said. "I had the weirdest dream. I was climbing up the mountain, see. I can't remember why, but it seemed urgent that I get to the top. There was a dragon, breathing fire, a fearsome sight, and there was a beautiful princess... Are you sure you're not laughing?"

"'Course not. Go on."

"Well, I've forgotten most of it, but Grampy was there too, looking so well and happy, not like he was before he died, all pale and old looking. Just before I woke up, I heard Grampy say, ‘Climb the mountain, Hugh.’ His voice faded away and I could hear it echo as though I were really at the top of Penrhys. ‘Climb... climb... climb...’ It was so real that I went straight to your window and looked up the mountain. Of course I couldn’t see Grampy but in some weird way I could still hear his voice. And I knew I had to do it even if it meant missing the Eisteddfod and making Mam angry.”

“Do you think Grampy was really trying to warn you? But if so, why did we end up trapped in this tunnel?” Megan sounded puzzled.

Hugh realized that in his own horror at being imprisoned in the tunnel he had wiped from his mind the cataclysmic sight of the school being swallowed up by the avalanche. If they’d gone to school they might have been buried in the school too. “We’ve probably got a better chance getting out of here. Though it seems a bit doubtful too. Oh, Meg, I wonder how many kids and teachers got away in time?”

Meg’s voice broke into his troubled thoughts. “Do you really *think* Grampy is alive somewhere, Heaven or some place, like they tell us in Sunday School?”

“If it is true, it makes sense that Grampy would want to help us, to warn us...” Hugh’s voice tailed off.

“It’s a bit creepy, though,” said Megan.

“I wouldn’t be scared of Grampy though, would you?” asked Hugh. He hugged his knees and laid his head on them, as he remembered Gramp’s jolly laugh and the beard that made him look like a thin Father Christmas. He had had to put a pillow inside his shirt when he dressed up for their Christmas party. How he wished Grampy hadn’t died!

Megan moved closer to Hugh and put out her hand to find one of his.

"What do you think about all that scary knocking?" she whispered. "I didn't want to say much for fear of frightening Iestyn. And did we really see those little men? Or was it all a nightmare? Is this part of the same dream? Maybe we'll wake up all safe in our own beds!"

Hugh felt his sister tremble. Indeed, a shudder deep inside him threatened to spread all through his body and escape in a loud scream. That would never do. *I'd wake the others and maybe bring the ceiling down on us.* Again he reminded himself that he was the oldest and must control himself. *Oh, God, please help me to be brave and get us out of this tunnel.*

As though reading her brother's mind, Megan said, "If we ever say our prayers, it better be now. Remember that psalm I read last Sunday in Sunday School? About lifting my eyes to the hills to get help from God? I wonder if He can help us when we're *inside* the hill?"

"I'm sure He can if we ask Him," said Hugh with a confidence he was far from feeling.

CHAPTER 9

After a short rest and a half-hearted attempt at a meal Peg and Ted Jenkins returned to the site where the school was buried.

"No sign of your young'uns yet," said Evan Howells, leaning on his shovel. "They've got a tunnel dug under the Infants' classrooms. They've found all the little ones." He nodded grimly towards the rows of covered stretchers. "They're starting on the Juniors now."

"Iestyn! Megan!" cried Peg, frantically. "I'll go there. You look for Hugh."

On his way to the far side of the mound Ted met Dr. Orr. He looked as though he had been up all night like the rest of them. His eyes were reddened, his cheeks pale with streaks of coal dust like the channels of black tears. He had brought most of Pontnewydd's children into the world, and worked as hard as any parent to save as many as possible from the cold, black dragon.

"Dai Thomas regained consciousness for a few minutes. I asked about Hugh and he said he wasn't there when he took attendance," the doctor said.

"That's funny. It's not like Hugh to be late for school."

Ted went back to Peg and shook his head. He didn't tell her that Hugh had not been in his classroom when the disaster occurred. What this meant he could not guess. Surely, if Hugh hadn't been in school they would have found him alive before this. He decided not to tell Peg until he'd talked to Hugh's teacher himself.

The digging was being done by professionals now. Relatives of the buried children and teachers stood in silent groups matching and waiting. Neighboring villages and places all over the world had sent help. Food for the teams of volunteer diggers and for the mourning families too. "It's like the soup kitchens we had during the strike," said Ivor Edwards. "Would to God it were only money and a living wage we're fighting for now, and not the lives of our children!"

There were three Protestant churches and one Catholic church in Pontnewydd. St. John's was the nearest to the school. Small differences forgotten, all denominations met together.

As Peg and Ted approached the cobbled path that led to the arched church door they saw a lurching form hesitating on its threshold.

"It's Glyn Roberts," they heard someone say. "First time he's been to church since his wife died."

"About time then. He finds his prayers at the bottom of a beer mug!"

The two women glared when Peg placed an admonitory finger on her lip.

Ted went and put a steadying hand on Glyn's sholder. "Come sit with us," he said. "Cyril's in our Megan's class, isn't he?"

After the service Peg invited Glyn to go home with them. With someone else to care for, Peg roused herself to wipe off the kitchen table and set it with a white cloth and dishes and cutlery. Visibly pulling himself together, Glyn took a sip of the hot, strong tea Peg poured from the big teapot with the glued-together lid. Brushing back the memory of Iestyn trying to help Mam with the dishes and dropping the lid out of his baby fingers, Peg handed the plate of wafer-tin bread slices lavishly spread with butter to their guest. Ted said, "Take some more ham, Glyn." With a guest to attend to, the Jenkins managed to eat their first meal since the disaster. The mines were to open again next day. They would close again for the community funeral for all the victims. This date was not yet set because there were many not accounted for.

"Maybe you can be taken on again, Glyn," said Ted. Glyn had been unemployed since the General Strike. With the mine behind schedule he might have a chance to go back.

"It's a judgment on me losing Cyril, too," burst out Glyn, as though he had held his feelings in too long and now they had to be expressed. "Since Mary died giving birth to him, I've had no time for the lad. My mother's had the bringing up to do, and she was never noted for her patience even when she was younger. Her never had much of a chance, did our Cyril!"

Ted looked at Peg. His torment was worse than theirs. What could they possibly say to ease it? He rose and put his hand on Glyn's shoulder. "Let's not give up yet. There's more digging to be done."

Hugh awoke with a start. In the blackness of the tunnel he had no idea what time it was. "Hey, Cyril, is your watch still working? Iestyn, let me have your torch a minute."

"I'll do it," said Iestyn sleepily.

"Keep it out of my eyes. You're blinding me! Shine it on the watch, stupid."

Cyril seemed his usual grumpy self again. Hugh stretched his stiffened body carefully.

"It's ten o'clock. Now is it last night or is it tomorrow morning? Or do I mean today?" Iestyn laughed. "Isn't it funny that days never stay the same? First they're yesterday, then today, and in no time at all they're tomorrow."

Cyril groaned. But Megan ignored him for once and answered Iestyn's cheerful chatter. "Well, yesterday seemed a month long. And a month of Sundays at that." Hugh crawled to the edge of the drop-off.

"Grab hold of my legs, will you while I see if the sky is still there." His eyes strained upward. "No, I don't need the torch. Save it for later, Iestyn." High above him Hugh could see a small patch of light. "It's a good thing that the shrine is in ruins, or we wouldn't be able to see the sky."

"Say, I'll bet that's why the miners stopped digging because this is a holy place," said Megan.

"More likely because it was too dangerous," said Cyril.

"I think you're right," said Hugh.

"D'you suppose there were miracles here, and people really did get healed," Iestyn said wistfully. And Hugh felt a pang of pain as he thought of Iestyn's useless legs.

"Well, do we go up or down?" asked Cyril.

"If only we had a rope," said Hugh. "How far down is it anyway?"

"I'll throw a little stone down and we can count the seconds it takes to hit the water. Ready?" said Megan. "One, two, three.." Megan's voice got to six before they heard a faint splash.

"Wow!" said Iestyn. "That's a long way!"

"I think we'd better try climbing up," said Hugh. "We've no means of knowing how deep the water is. And it's too dark to see whether there's a ledge or something to stand on down there."

By the light of the torch, noticeably fainter now, the children studied the wall of the well. It was built of irregularly shaped stones which offered the possibility of shallow foot holds and hand holds. It looked slimy and wet and, as Hugh discovered when he stretched out his hand, damp and cold to the touch.

"Wish my feet still worked," said Iestyn. "I don't think I could climb up." And he whistled a sad and tuneless song.

"We'll need your strong shoulders though," said Hugh putting his hand on his brother's arm. "We'd never have dug Meg out in time without you."

"It just needs one of us to climb up," said Megan thoughtfully. "Then go for ropes and help to pull the others out."

"Not me," said Cyril quickly.

"I'll go," said Hugh, calculating the distance between the jutting stones. The climb up the wet wall looked more impossible the longer he looked at it. He decided to start before common sense told him it was too risky. "Make a back, Cyril, and I'll climb on your shoulders."

"We'll keep you steady," said Iestyn. "Come on, Meg, you take the other side."

After wobbling precariously on Cyril's shoulders, Hugh grabbed for his first hand hold. He swayed and Cyril shouted, "We're falling, and yelped as Hugh grabbed his hair. Megan reached to hold Hugh, while Iestyn braced Cyril's knees.

"Sorry, Cyril," said Hugh as he recovered his balance and stood up leaning with both hands on the wall. Gripping projecting stones, Hugh moved one metal tipped boot into a small chink, kicking and scraping it until it was big enough for a foot hold. He moved that foot back on Cyril's shoulder for a fraction of a second and then, with a "Here goes!" he propelled himself with a sudden, smooth springing movement upward into the well. To his relief his left hand grasped a projecting stone he'd seen above the one he held with his right hand.

There Hugh stayed, spread-eagled flat against the wall. His fingers felt wet and cold and Hugh feared they would slip off the stones. Very carefully he let go his right hand and wiped it carefully on his trousers. He knew he was postponing the dread move from this first uneasy position. He looked determinedly ahead before his courage failed him. Shifting his balance smoothly because the slightest error or jerky movement could send him hurtling down to the water below, he moved his right hand to a new peg of stone, being careful to keep a firm grasp on his left hand hold. He tested the new stone and found it safe. His two arms were spread out, one above the other, his face so close to the stones that he found it difficult to look up without risking his safe grip on the hand holds. The rough edges of the stones chafed his cheeks.

"Just like a bloody fly," he thought.

"To the left of your right hand, and two inches up," whispered Megan. "Strike a match, Cyril. The torch is no good now."

Hugh was so flattened to the wall that all he could see was a grey blur. Afraid to turn his head he managed to lift his cheek from the stones just enough to see where Meg directed him. Slowly, he stretched his fingers until his grip on the new peg was secure.

"Put your feet where your hands were," called Iestyn.

Trouble is, I don't have eyes in my toes, thought Hugh, and then the idea struck him so funny he had an almost uncontrollable desire to laugh. He hung, arms and legs outspread, and forced himself to stifle the giggles which would indubitably upset his balance. He concentrated all his thoughts on his next move. First his right foot where his right hand had been, and then his left foot found a resting place. Maybe, instead of moving his hands and then his feet, he should move a hand and a foot alternately. He deliberately refrained from looking up to the patch of daylight that was his goal. He kept his mind on one hand, then one foot, then the other hand and foot.

I'm more like a caterpillar than a fly, Hugh thought as he felt his body flatten out, and them hump up, and then stretch out full length again.

The silence seemed a solid thing, almost as solid as the stone wall that was at once his prison and his means of escape. Suddenly Hugh felt a strange indentation as he groped for a hand hold with his left hand. It felt almost like a face. A small protruberance shaped like a nose. Below it, a hollow for a mouth. Above it, two smaller holes in the right position for eyes. He had to look. Carefully he raised his head and saw a horrifying visage carved right into the stone. The eye cavities were malevolent slits that seemed to mock him. In the shadows the protruding tongue seemed to move and for one frenzied moment Hugh thought the face was contorting to spit at him. Instinctively Hugh recoiled and with a spattering of small stones and dirt he felt himself falling. Arms and legs outspread, still in his position for climbing, he plummeted down. A wrenching cry he didn't recognize as his, tapered off into a mighty splash. Hugh found himself deep below the surface of the water at the bottom of the well.

CHAPTER 10

One of the tunnels collapsed, burying the rescuers under the heavy wet mud. Frantic digging by everyone enabled them to be pulled out in time. Bruised and wet, their faces as black as if they were working down the mine, they were carried off by the ambulance to the hospital.

After what seemed an interminable time under water, Hugh felt himself floating to surface. Something touched his arm and then veered off. A monster? A giant fish? The Big Worm from the Mabinogion tales? Hugh's blood seemed to freeze in horror. He could see it approaching again. Nowhere to escape. Diving 'd be no good. Suddenly he saw it clearly. It was Iestyn's crutch!

Shouting exultantly, he grabbed it. The water was so cold, and the fear had been so intense, Hugh had trouble breathing. Now he could hold on without danger of sinking, and catch his breath. After a brief rest, he kicked his legs, using his right arm as a paddle, and manoeuvered himself to the side of the well where he could see three small figures peering down at him.

"Yoooooooh," he shouted. "I'm safe." He could see their arms waving in joyful greeting.

Now what? Holding on to the crutch with one hand, and a knob of rock with the other, Hugh dangled his legs as far down the wall as they could go without submerging his face. No ledge or shelf. Just wall as far down as his feet could reach. Was it worth submerging his head again to probe further. The well must end somewhere. Or could it be a bottomless pit?

Here goes, Hugh thought, taking a deep breath and forcing his body downward. He held on to the crutch which would help him float back up. His kicking feet, heavy in his boots, found a hole. Using his arms he swam down to it and found it broadened out at one end. His breath was giving out when he felt his feet land on solid ground. His lungs began to hurt and Hugh had to decide whether to go back to the surface or pursue this apparent tunnel. Letting go of the crutch, he swam along the passage and to his great relief found the floor sloped upward until he was soon out of the water.

Groping around in the darkness he discovered he was in a tunnel of the same width as of the mining tunnel. Even by jumping he could not reach a ceiling, if there was one. He crawled along the floor on his hands and knees and came to a step that led upward. Then another, and another. How he wished he had Iestyn's weak torch or one of Cyril's matches. When he had counted seven steps, Hugh sat on the top one to rest. Water was still dripping down his legs but now he was not moving he became more conscious of the cold and discomfort. His heart was still pumping wildly and every breath was painful. But he was alive!

He proceeded along the passage until he came to an obstruction. Feeling around it he discovered it was a door. I hope it's not locked, he thought. He tugged one way and then the other and the door, for such it was, swung towards him, almost knocking him down the steps. The creaking of its hinges might have heralded the egress of a monster long caged in this subterranean room, the sound was so unearthly and loud.

Hugh felt he could not go on alone. He'd been through too much. Besides the others would be worrying about him. They might think he had drowned. He must go back and show himself. Every cell in his body objected to plunging back into the chilly water. But it had to be done. Their only hope of escape lay through the door he had just discovered. Since he had failed to climb to the top of the well it did not seem likely that the others could. It was impossible for Iestyn. Megan would have enough spunk to try, she was as good as any boy in many ways, but her arms might not be muscular enough. And what if she fell? She might not be as lucky as he'd been. She might hit her head against the wall. What about Cyril? He could be wrong, as he'd shown flashes of more common sense than he'd thought him capable of, but no, he didn't think Cyril would want to try it.

Flinching as the cold water filled his boots and climbed up his legs, Hugh took a deep breath and plunged in. He swam until he felt the opposite wall and then forced himself upward. He should have taken his heavy boots off, he thought. His head bobbed above the water and he reached for the friendly crutch which kept bumping into him and backing off only to nuzzle him again much as a welcoming pet might.

From above he could hear vague shouts. Three small figures were jumping up and down and pointing in his direction.

Cupping his mouth with his hands to direct the sound, he hollered, "You must jump down!" And watched their movements stop abruptly. "Jump. It's the only way..." He could hear his voice reverberating and swirling from side to side of the old well. He imagined their saying, "Never!" or Megan's "Has he lost his mind?" and smiled despite the cold.

"One at a time. Come on. Hurry..."

Hugh hadn't been this wet since he'd gone with Dad to the Association football play-offs at Wembley. Wales against Scotland. They'd sat there in the rain with newspapers over their heads which hadn't done much good to keep them dry. The players were sliding around in the mud. The ball was muddy and each time a player headed it his forehead got muddy too. What a day! Wales had won, and the fans had streamed over the field, ripping up the goal posts, and lifting the players on their shoulders. No-one seemed to care about being wet in the triumph of victory. Well, he minded now! Why didn't they hurry and jump, and get it over with.

He was chilled to the marrow, whatever that was. Something inside bones, he thought. From some recess of memory he dredged an old rhyme.

> Taffy was a Welshman, Taffy was a thief
> Taffy came to my house and stole a leg of beef.
> I went to Taffy's house and Taffy wasn't home.
> Taffy came to my house and stole a marrow bone.

He wished he was in anybody's house. Anywhere but here, soaking wet, with the prospect of three more plunges to the underground tunnel, each time with a reluctant swimmer to take care of.

Hugh waved and shouted once more to spur them on, but they seemed to be talking animatedly and he couldn't hear a word.

He hated that old nursery rhyme. Taffy was a thief, indeed! Hugh's mother had told him it was written years ago by invaders of Wales. There had been many battles and the Welsh had often left their homes and been driven to the mountain caves. Of course, they came on raids to their former homes and tried to harass the enemy and drive them out! He wondered why Taffy had become a nickname for a Welshman. Only the English used it, and it was always said with a bit of a sneer. Maybe they were trying to say 'Dafydd' the way the Welsh said it, and 'Taffy' was the closest they could get. He shrugged and felt the water cover his nose. He'd forgotten where he was for a minute. What were they doing up there? He uttered a howl that finally got some action. He saw Iestyn crawl to the edge and wave, then tuck his lifeless feet under him. Hugh watched as he started rocking to propel himself into position but he couldn't seem to force himself beyond the overhang. Hugh hoped he wouldn't scrape against the edge. Then he saw Megan and Cyril push him.

Megan's wail echoed eerily but Hugh's attention was focussed on Iestyn, who hit the water with a resounding splash, and then came floundering to the surface. Hugh held out the crutch and saw the gleam of Iestyn's teeth as he reached for his old friend.

"Safe!" yelled Hugh. "Wait 'til I signal. Wait," he repeated more loudly. "Don't jump yet!"

Hugh explained to Iestyn about swimming under water to the tunnel opening. Fortunately he was a good swimmer. After his illness he had swum regularly to stimulate his leg muscles. There had been no lasting improvement, but Iestyn had learned to love the water where he could move as fast as anyone. Holding the crutch between them, first Hugh, and then Iestyn swam down and through the passageway. When they crawled to the steps Iestyn took off his jacket and as he twisted it Hugh could hear the water trickling. "I'll wring out yours too," he said to Hugh. And Hugh remembered then to take off his boots, and socks.

Back at the well, Hugh yelled, "Crutch", waving the crutch he had. Then, "Matches!", hoping they'd find some way to keep them dry.

To Hugh's surprise, Megan and Cyril held on to each other around the waist as though they were going to dance, and stepped off the edge together.

The two figures separated in mid-air and collided as they hit the water. Hugh squeezed against the wall to get out of their way, and held one crutch to Megan who was the first to surface. A second or two later, Cyril came sputtering up and grabbed for the other crutch. The three of them bobbed together in the dark water while Hugh explained what they had to do to get to the dry passage.

"I'm not much of a swimmer," said Cyril.

"You'll be fine," said Hugh. "Just hang on to the crutch."

Hugh saw Meg reach out and pat Cyril's shoulder. "Don't worry," she said, "Hugh will get us through." Meg being nice to Cyril? Hugh couldn't believe it.

With two crutches he would only have to swim underwater one more time. "Meg, you keep the first crutch between you and me, and the second crutch between you and Cyril, and we'll keep together. Just like a chain of human sea-weed." he said, feeling jaunty.

"Just take a deep breath, and don't let go of your crutch. Ready?"

When Hugh and Megan reached the safety of the steps, Meg noticed that the second crutch trailed loosely behind her. "Cyril's not here," she gasped.

CHAPTER 11

The line of green hills encircled the village as they had since prehistoric times. Without the huge dragon-shaped head they no longer resembled a green serpent body.

Would to God it was still there, thought Glyn. And that Cyril was safe home in bed. He'd never spent much time with him and now it was too late. He pounded his fist against the lamppost, and didn't even feel the pain in his bruised fingers.

Hugh sprang to his feet, "I'll find Cyril," he cried. Stumbling over his boots in the darkness, he made his way for the fourth time back to the well. If only I hadn't saved myself that extra trip! I'm having to do it anyway, and now Cryil may be dead! He plunged back into the cold water and kicked his way to the surface. No Cyril! Hugh had hoped to find him floating there. He must be caught on a rock or something below. Unconscious or... He pushed the unpleasant thought away for the second time. But it seemed to hover at the back of his mind like a sinister specter.

Two dives and still no sign of Cyril. Suddenly Hugh felt someone swimming beside him and hope surged through him. No, it was Iestyn. Good for you, brother, he thought. Down they dived, and this time Hugh felt Cyril's body lying just below the junction of the passage and the well. With Iestyn's help he pulled Cyril to the safety of the dry floor.

Cyril was still breathing. Hugh turned him on his stomach. It was so hard in the dark to do the procedures he had learned at the St. John's Ambulance course. He pushed at where he thought the small of Cyril's back was until he heard water spatter out of Cyril's mouth and trickle into the puddle made from their wet clothes.

Then, rhythmically and evenly, he kept pushing and relaxing until his arms were tired. "Come take a turn," he yelled to Iestyn and Megan. He'd practised on them when he was working for his badge so they knew what they had to do.

Suddenly, Cyril moved, and uttered a faint groan. "I thought I was a goner!" he said softly.

Megan pulled off his sodden jacket, and rubbed his arms to warm them.

"I hit my head on the side of the passage," he said, still lying down, but on his back. Hugh could guess how it happened. Being the last, Cyril had swung out as he held the second crutch. He never should have taken two of them at once!

Megan said quickly, "It's no-one's fault. It was a good idea. I should have let Cyril go next to Hugh! If anyone's to blame, it's me."

Hugh marveled again how sensitive his sister was, even to the thoughts he did not put into words.

"It's *my* fault. I'm so clumsy," said Cyril.

"Oh, no, you're not," said Megan swiftly. "I shall always be grateful for your spurring me on, when I thought I just *couldn't* jump. And suggesting we jump together.

"Well," said Cyril, "I was just as scared as you. So it helped me, too."

"And you had the idea to tie the matches in my scarf, so they wouldn't get wet. Where's the second crutch anyway?" said Megan.

"I wondered why your scarf was tied to the crutch," said Iestyn. "I untied it right away to wring it out with the other clothes. I didn't notice any matches, just a paper bag that was only wet around the edges."

"I stuck the box in with the left over sandwiches," said Cyril. "I hope they aren't soggy."

"I forgot about the one in my pocket. The one you gave us last night. I'm not as smart as you, Cyril," said Hugh. "If I'd taken it out as soon as I found this passage it probably would have been all right."

"I'll take it, soggy or not," cried Iestyn. "I'm starved."

"Yum, *almost* like Mam's bread and milk." Iestyn sucked at the wet mixture. "Who else wants a bite? Or a soggy mouthful."

"Ugh," said Hugh. "More like bread and water, or wallpaper paste."

"Let's each eat a mouthful anyway," said Megan. "When we get to a place where we can see what we're doing we'll have a party and eat the two good sandwiches. I'm so glad you took them off the crutch before we dragged it through the water again."

Guiding the wet pieces of disintegrating bread from the bag to their mouths was a difficult business. Hugh felt it smearing his chin, and he pushed the wet crumbs into his mouth with his fingers. "It's a good thing we're in the dark," said Megan with a giggle.

"What about the matches?" asked Hugh.

"The box feels a bit damp, but the inside may be all right," said Iestyn. "I didn't open it."

"Well, if Cyril feels well enough to move on," said Hugh, "let's wait till we're through the mysterious doorway before we light one. No use wasting 'em. If the door doesn't lead to the outdoors we may all be goners!" Hugh wished he could bite the words back. But that was how he felt. He was tired of keeping up a show of courage when he was cold, wet, and scared.

Feeling their way in the dark, the four children moved slowly and tentatively along the black corridor. At the steps, Hugh felt Iestyn, who was next to him, move downwards to sit on the steps. He lost his footing and stepped back on one foot, landing on Iestyn's fingers. A howl from Iestyn and a muttered apology from Hugh broke the silence.

"I can't use my crutches on these steps so watch it!"

"I wish I *could* watch," snapped Hugh. "This darkness is getting to me!" Losing my temper is no good, thought Hugh. But I can't help being grouchy. Enough is enough. His outstretched hands scraped the closed door.

"I'm at the door. I'll swing it open. Be careful it doesn't knock you down the steps."

With a loud unearthly screech the heavy wooden door swung past Hugh. Ahead was still solid blackness. "Let's everybody get to the top of the steps and then we'll try a match," said Hugh, his heart beating so fast he could scarcely get the words out.

Hugh felt Iestyn swing himself on to the top step. "That was better than crawling like a worm," he said. "I tried my torch a while back. No light at all, just a glimmer that faded just as I looked at it."

Now that Iestyn was out of the way, Megan, then Cyril arrived in a rush.

"I'm afraid the box is too damp to strike the match," said Cyril.

"Try the stone step," said Hugh, "but be careful to find a place we haven't dripped on."

"There's only three matches left, so I'd better be careful," muttered Cyril. "Here goes!"

The three Jenkins children waited quietly. Better not grumble at Cyril or give him advice, thought Hugh, or he might lose his temper and maybe waste a precious match.

Light flared and the slightly sulphurous smell made Hugh's nostrils quiver. Ahead of them was a large room. There were no windows. There were shelves on all the walls. Rows and rows of bottles stood on the shelves like sentinels on guard. A refectory table covered with dust was in the middle of the room. Upon it, festooned with cobwebs, was a pewter candlestick. Hugh dashed over and picked it up. "There's a candle in it," he shouted. "Quick, Cyril!"

"Ouch," cried Cyril, as the match burned his fingers and went out.

"Before you try another match, Cyril, I'll try to dig out the wick. It's buried solid in the wax."

"Let me try," said Megan, "my fingernails are longer than yours."

"I think I've got it," said Hugh. "It's so hard doing everything in the dark."

"Here goes," said Cyril, and Hugh heard the scrape across the stone floor and then saw the flame that chased the darkness back into the corners. Now if only it would light the candle they'd be able to explore and maybe find a way out.

Cyril cupped his hand carefully around the flickering flame and slowly held it over the candle. The wick caught, and after a spurt of wildly dancing light, the candle gave off a steady flame. Hugh sighed with relief. He looked around. What a sorry looking crew they were! Megan's red dress dripped stains down her arms and legs. Her jacket had picked up dust and dirt where she had trailed it behind her along the passageway. Being wet, it had picked up everything. I guess mine's just as dirty, he thought. Cyril looked pale. His lips looked blue, almost black. There was a lump on his forehead. Iestyn's red hair was pasted down over his eyes, not sticking up in spikes as it usually did. Hugh looked down at his trousers. There were holes at the knees, and a long tear down one leg. His Sunday best! But they were still alive. That was the most important thing. Mam wouldn't care about his trousers when she knew they were safe. Would they ever be safe? They'd come through many dangers but would they ever find a way out and get home? They were wet, hungry, but able to move on. But where?

CHAPTER 12

"They mustn't give up," cried Peg. "They must find our children."

"They're just stopping for a rest, Peg. They've been at it hours."

Volunteers from neighboring towns brought sandwiches and hot tea and coffee for the tired workers.

Hugh shook off his feeling of exhaustion and looked around the room. There were no windows so it must be a cellar of some kind. There should be a door, but he couldn't see one except the one that led to the well.

"There must be a door leading into this place. The one we came through just goes to the well," Hugh said. "Maybe there's one in the opposite corner, behind those shelves." Hugh tried to move the shelves which were not fastened to the wall but a portable unit that covered the wall space from the floor almost to the ceiling.

"Wait," cried Megan, "let's move the bottles first."

"What's in 'em? Pop?" asked Iestyn. "What wouldn't I give for some of Mrs. Lewis's small beer that we always drink at Sunday dinner."

"Or sarsparilla," said Cyril smacking his lips.

"My favorite is orange squash," said Megan.

"Well, I'd settle for some clear, cold water from the Spout," said Hugh. "This dust makes me feel I'm choking."

"Well," said Iestyn, "I just may have some. I filled up my bottle on the way up the mountain."

All four children took a drink out of Iestyn's bottle, and continued their task of moving the dusty bottles from the shelves to the floor.

"What's inside 'em, anyway?" asked Cyril, knocking the neck of one of them on the stone floor so that it broke and some of the contents spilled out. The children clustered around. "Smells like vinegar," said Megan. "No orange squash, worse luck."

"Hey, there *is* a door here," shouted Hugh. "Come on, help me move the shelves out of the way!"

The children dragged the shelves far enough from the wall so that they could squeeze behind them.

The heavy wooden door seemed immovable. It seemed cemented into the wall by grey matted cobwebs. Hugh ran his fingers across the lower edges and the cobwebs came away easily from the door but stuck to his hands in long stringy chains. "Ugh, like handcuffs," said Megan. "Here, let's use these 3-legged stools to climb on to get them off the top of the door."

Soon the door's outline was revealed, but there didn't seem to be a knob, or any way of opening it. There seemed to be a bar on the other side that kept it firmly closed. Hugh went over to the door they had found open at the top of the steps. Yes, it was just like the second door, and he could see that the bar fitted through some metal slots just like his leather belt at the top of his trousers.

Going back to the closed door where the three others were trying without success to pry it open, he said, "Maybe we can find something narrow to push the bar backwards."

They emptied their pockets and used a varied collection, a pencil, a scout knife, and a comb, but to no avail. Megan's comb snapped in two.

They sat on the stools which they had found around the refectory table and surveyed their situation. "It's like one of those puzzles where each box has a smaller one inside it and just when you think you've found the surprise, you find another box," said Hugh, with a sigh.

"At least our boxes are getting bigger," said Megan. "But how we're going to get out of this one, beats me!"

"I'm hungry," said Iestyn. "Can't we eat those last two sandwiches now?"

"Two sandwiches. Thanks for sharing, Cyril," said Megan. "That's half each."

"Not exactly a feast," said Cyril. "I wish I hadn't been so greedy, gobbling the others so fast."

"How come you had so much food?" asked Iestyn. "Were you planning to be away a week?"

"Why didn't we bring more food?" said Hugh.

"That's because you aren't used to mitching school the way I do," said Cyril. "I hole up all day and sometimes I'm too late for supper. If Gran has washed the dishes, I'm out of luck, so I take plenty of food with me."

I can't imagine Mam being like that, thought Hugh. She might scold a bit, but she'd never let us go to bed hungry. Poor Cyril.

"Thanks for sharing, Cyril," said Megan.

"Thanks for saving my life," said Cyril, gruffly. "I'd have drowned back there if you hadn't come back for me."

Hugh felt embarrassed. "You'd have done the same for us, Cyril."

Megan nibbled small pieces of her half sandwich and chewed with determination. "You counting or what?" asked Iestyn curiously.

"Well, now's the time to do what Dad says Mr. Gladstone did. Chew every mouthful thirty-two times. Makes it last."

"Probably makes your jaws so tired you think you've eaten a whole meal," said Hugh, with a sigh.

"Say, Cyril, why *do* you mitch all the time?" said Megan curiously. "School isn't so bad, really. With your brains, you'd be top of the class if you went every day."

Cyril stopped chewing, and even in the shadowy candle-light Hugh could see that his face turned red.

"Maybe I will if I have friends like you there," he said, his voice so low that Hugh could hardly hear him. Megan did, though, because she turned a bit red, too, and instead of making her usual teasing retort she jumped up and said, "Come on, let's tackle that door again now we've eaten such a big meal."

"What we really ought to do is take our wet clothes off, and try to dry them," said Hugh, looking around for something to change into. "What are those brown things hanging over there?"

The children ran to a wall that had wooden pegs from which hung loosely-woven woollen cloaks. Megan got to them first, and held one out before her in disdain. "Dusty and full of moth holes!" she said.

"Don't shake it near me," cried Iestyn, and promptly sneezed.

"Better than wet clothes," Hugh said. "I'm going to strip and put one on." "We can hang our wet clothes from these pegs. If we stay in them any longer we'll get TB, or at least a bad cold."

Megan hesitated, and then laughed. "Hugh, you look like a monk with that cowl over your head. We'll all be monks and pretend it's Hallowe'en!"

The robe smelled musty and trailed along the ground. Hugh hitched it up around the rope belt until he could walk without tripping over it. He looked up to see three other scruffy looking monks peeping out from under their hoods.

"Now, you'd all better behave. Be dignified, and remember to say your prayers," said Hugh, with a laugh.

"I've been praying inside my head, all along," said Megan. "Why do you suppose we're still all right?" Her eyes twinkled mischievously.

"Who found the passage and pulled you all through?" said Hugh, not liking Megan claiming all the credit.

"Well, like Dad says, 'God works through us'," said Iestyn.

"Say," said Cyril, with surprise in his voice, "I just thought. This must be part of the old monastery on the top of Penrhys!"

"Gee, maybe we've discovered something no-one has seen for years!" said Megan. "This dust is history." And she wrote her name on the table.

"History or not, it still makes me sneeze," said Iestyn, holding his brown sleeve over his nose. "Choo!" he erupted. "There's more dust in my robe than on the table."

"Certainly feels better than my wet dress," said Megan, taking it off the pegs and shaking it. "Will our clothes dry in here?"

"Come on, let's tackle the door again," said Hugh. "It seems to be our only hope of getting out of here."

He held the candle and they studied the problem of opening the door.

"Look, there are more candles," shouted Iestyn.

"Good, we'll keep one lit all the time," said Hugh.

Cyril warned, "There's only one match left."

"We've got to keep a candle lit at all times." Hugh shuddered at the thought of being in total blackness again.

Hugh joined Megan who was studying the hinges. "They're very rusty. Maybe we can loosen them and get the door open that way?"

"Yes, the metal looks quite corroded in places," said Hugh. "Maybe we can rub them so they'll fall apart."

"Mam uses vinegar to clean things," said Megan.

"Hey, that spoiled wine smelled like vinegar. Let's use that," cried Iestyn, who hobbled on his crutches over where the broken flagon lay. The shadows made him look like a giant bird, thought Hugh. Yet, he never acted crippled. He hadn't slowed them down much, except at the beginning of the avalanche. Suddenly, he remembered the well and its reputation for healing. What if?... Miracles don't happen today, he thought. Did they ever?

"Come on, Hugh." Megan was already scrubbing away at the rusty hinges. "I'm using one of my socks."

The rubbing had little effect upon the hinges but it did get Hugh's circulation moving and he felt warm for the first time since he fell into the well water. "I'm hot," said Megan.

"Let's have a rest," said Cyril.

"I bag the table," yelled Megan. "There might be mice, or rats."

"No sign of droppings that I can see, though there's so much dirt in the corners it's hard to tell."

"No food either for them or us," said Iestyn, with a sigh. "All that exercise makes me hungry."

"Don't talk about food. It must be suppertime." And Hugh thought of the kitchen table loaded with Ma's good cooking, and the black-leaded kettle with its brass lid rattling up and down as steam poured out of the spout.

Fish and chips...Sausage and mashed potatoes...Faggots and peas... He could even enjoy those minced liver burgers! In desperation to block these mental tortures he changed the subject. "What is the time, Cyril?"

"My watch's had it. It stopped while I was under water, I expect."

"So we've no means of knowing if it's night or day," said Hugh.

"It must be bedtime," said Iestyn. "Funny thing, I never wanted to go to bed when I was home, but oh, how I'd love to go there now."

"Well, let's curl up like last night, and get some shut-eye," said Hugh. Was it really only one night ago that they slept in the mine tunnel before he climbed up the well, and fell? Hugh shuddered as he felt again the lurching terror of dropping from the top of the well to the bottom. Yes, he'd almost been at the top. He could remember the large circle of light that seemed to draw him in, and the parapet that was within his grasp. Suddenly, he saw again the grimacing face that had caused him to lose his grip. He trembled.

"Are you all right, Hugh?" asked Megan, far above him, as she lay on the table.

He forced himself to answer. He'd have liked to tell then about the evil stone image but it would only scare them here in this shadowy prison, and they would not be able to escape for a few hours into peaceful sleep. He hoped he could stop thinking of all the terrible things that had happened since they had left home so light-heartedly two days ago. It seemed more like a week. He turned on his other side. The stone floor was cold and hard.

"Yes, Meg. Just sleepy, that's all. Goodnight all."

A chorus of 'Night night', and 'Sleep tight', and Cyril's "May the bedbugs bite," succumbed to a silence that held no peace in it. There was a tension in the dusty air, an expectation of further mishaps. Hugh guessed that the others were thinking back over their fearful experiences. Oh, God, he'd forgotten the school and what had happened to it! How could he have been remembering his own troubles without giving a thought to Mr. Thomas, his teacher, and all his butties? Where they already dead? He tossed and turned restlessly. He found himself thinking of the prayer his mother had taught them:

> "Lord, keep us safe this night, secure from all our fears.
> May angels guard us while we sleep, Till morning light appears."

He remembered the dream in which his grandfather had come to warn him. Oh, Grampy, he sighed. And fell asleep.

CHAPTER 13

Preparations for a mass funeral for all the victims of the avalanche were being made in Pontnewydd. All the children had not been found. But they were presumed dead. One sunny day followed another. Tears of rain fell silently indoors. But life went on, not quite as usual. The surviving children had no desire to play. The colliers went back to work. But there was no singing.

Hugh awoke from a pleasant dream. He felt relaxed and happy. But as soon as he realized where he was, terror returned, and the happy episode, whatever it was, was erased from his mind as chalk from a blackboard. The class. The school. All the nightmare that was all the more horrible because it was real. It had actually happened. He saw again the monster mud pounce upon the school. And it had disappeared. Hugh opened his eyes because, however gloomy the underground room was it was safer than his memory of the avalanche. He looked up where Megan slept on top of the table. Her hand hung down, limp and somehow helpless. He shook his foolish thought away. Megan was never helpless. She could always think of something practical to do. She was fun, too, though this long ordeal had taken a lot out of her. He looked across at Iestyn, lying beside him. He looked as though he were smiling in his sleep. Hugh hadn't wanted to pull his cart up the mountain. What if he'd left him behind to go to the doomed schoolhouse? He never would have forgiven himself. But they weren't safe yet. They might never get out... Cyril was breathing heavily. He'd had a lucky escape. Didn't sound as though he had much attention at home.

I suppose there was always some reason that certain kids were nuisances. Now he'd got to know Cyril, he wasn't so bad. He'd be greedy if he hadn't been forced to share with his younger brother and sister. Not that he always wanted to.

Suddenly, he felt rather than saw a movement. Was Megan getting up? No, her hand was still hanging down. The candle flickered and Hugh raised himself on one elbow to see if it had almost burned out. No, there was still about an inch of wax left. It must have been a shadow I saw, Hugh thought. He looked more closely. There stood a figure clothed in a robe and hood like the ones they had put on. There did not seem to be a face, but maybe the face was shrouded in the shadow cast by the hood. Hugh froze, afraid to breathe. It seemed to sense Hugh's terror. With a thin white hand it made the sign of the cross on its chest and then pointed upward to the ceiling. Then it floated up where it pointed, and disappeared.

His heart pounding, Hugh was afraid to move. Then he heard a querulous voice. "Hugh, I'm scared." It was Megan. Had she seen it, too? He sprang up and grabbed her hand, now in front of her eyes not hanging below the table top. "Did you see it?" he hissed. "Tell me what you saw!"

It hadn't been a dream. Megan had seen it too. She described the figure of the monk exactly as Hugh had seen it. He ran to the shelf and got another candle. And another. They must have more light. Leaving the one that had lit the room while they slept still burning in its puddle of wax, Hugh and Megan lit two others from it and each holding one they looked all around the eerie chamber, into every corner, behind each set of shelves. There was no-one there but the four of them.

"It must have been a ghost," said Megan. "We couldn't both have dreamed the same dream."

Hugh gulped. “Well, it didn’t harm us. I wonder why it pointed to the ceiling.” He raised his candle high. “Look,” he shouted. “A square crack! Could it be...?”

“A trapdoor!” Megan yelled, waking Iestyn and Cyril, who sat up and yawned.

Hugh, Megan and Cyril sprang on the table and tried to reach the ceiling. Hugh jumped down and grabbed one of the stools. Cyril snatched it from him and stood on it. Hugh let out a howl of protest. Cyril scrambled off it quickly. He couldn’t reach the ceiling, and he’d never seen Hugh so angry. Hugh hopped on the stool as it wobbled on the table top. Stretching to his full height, ready to spring to the floor if his wobbly perch deserted him, he was able only to touch the ceiling.

“I think you need me,” said Iestyn.

Cyril and Megan helped haul him up on the table. “You won’t need the stool. I’ll climb on Hugh’s shoulders. Should be close enough to push it up.”

With his muscular shoulders, Iestyn could do it, too, Hugh thought. “It may be stiff,” he warned, “hasn’t been used in years, by the look of it.”

“Here, take this piece of comb, and scrape the dirt and cobwebs out of the crack,” said Megan.

Hugh parted his feet to make a firmer base to hold Iestyn’s weight. He was glad he didn’t have to stand on the wobbly stool. Though they might need it if Iestyn’s estimate was wrong. Soon, Iestyn’s feet were dangling on his chest. He could feel their coldness right through his robe. They were bare, and dirty. Like my own, Hugh thought, but he dare not look down to see.

“It *is* stiff,” gasped Iestyn.

“Maybe it’s bolted on the other side, like the door,” said Cyril.

Hugh groaned. "Am I too heavy?" asked Iestyn.

"No, keep trying. Push as hard as you can," he said, hoping Cyril's sensible suspicion was wrong.

Suddenly, Iestyn shouted, "It's beginning to move. Think I'm pushing at the wrong end. Can you turn and face the other way?"

Megan held on to Iestyn as Hugh turned. "Wish us luck," cried Iestyn as he pushed upward once more. With a groan the wooden trap door was wrenched up and fell out of sight with a crash. "Pass me up a candle," said Iestyn. Placing the candle holder on the floor above him, he held on and lifted his body to the room above.

"Nothing but ruins, stones and mess," he shouted to the others. "Not even room to stand up. Wait, there's stairs going down." His face peered down at them from the square opening.

Hugh thought fast. It didn't seem worth it to climb after Iestyn if there wasn't a way out. "Where are the steps?" he asked and when Iestyn pointed, "That's where the door is down here. Can you get down and try to open it?" Iestyn did not answer but Hugh could hear him moving in that direction, throwing rocks or objects out of his way as he went.

The three went over to the door and waited. "I never thought about it before, but why were the shelves pulled in front of this door?"

"To keep someone out?" asked Cyril.

"Someone escaped by hiding in this storeroom," said Megan.

"And after barricading himself inside, his enemy locked him in here by pushing the bar across. Well then, where did he go? Out through the well? Or..." Hugh thought of the ghostly monk. Did he die here when the air gave out? Or of starvation? Did he drown in the well, or did he climb out as

Hugh tried to do? Maybe he had friends who lowered a rope down for him.

Soft slithering sounds as Iestyn moved down the steps sitting down on each one and swinging himself to the next one as Hugh had often seen him do at home heralded his arrival at the other side of the door.

Slowly the bar moved and the heavy door swung away from them with a groan. Where was Iestyn? Hugh dashed through. Iestyn was sitting on a step, his head in his hands. He looked up. "I couldn't reach the bar without climbing on the steps," he said. "And then it was hard..."

"Iestyn, you're a hero," he cried. "You got it open. You set us free!"

CHAPTER 14

The news of the Pontnewydd disaster brought money and offers of help from all over the world. People everywhere wept for the parents of the small Welsh village. The children were in God's hands.

Megan cried out when she saw Iestyn's scratched hands and bleeding feet. "I had to squeeze past rocks and stuff. I'm all right!"

"I'll get your crutches," said Cyril. "And what about your shoes? Are they dry enough to wear?"

None of the clothes had dried. Hugh had become used to the musty odor of his monk's robe. It was full of holes but warm because it was made of homespun wool. The monks had probably tended sheep on Penrhys mountain, ancestors of the ones that scrounged the village streets for food when they got tired of browsing the mountain slopes. He looked around the room they had just stepped into. Each of them held a candle so it was illuminated fairly well.

"It's still part of the cellar of the old monastery. Another box in the puzzle. There's a fireplace, and a door. "No," said Megan, who had run ahead of the others. "It's just an archway. And it's all filled in."

"You mean there's no way out?" cried Cyril.

"It looks as though the monastery fell in so there's probably no way we can get to the surface," said Hugh. "We're stuck here forever." He was too tired and discouraged to keep cheerful. To think they had struggled through so many dangers only to find their escape blocked. Here they were, buried inside a mountain, with a ton of stones from a ruined monastery on top of them. Hugh lay down on the dusty floor and closed his eyes.

"What's that against the wall?" Megan's voice broke into Hugh's gloomy thoughts. She ran over and pulled some old pieces of sacking away from the wooden paneling. "Oh," she exclaimed. The others gathered around.

It was an oil painting. In the center was a huge oak tree and, caught in its branches, was a statue. "It's Mary and Jesus, when he was a baby," cried Iestyn.

"You're right. It's like the one we saw in the museum at Cardiff," said Megan. "But what's it doing up in a tree?"

"Look," said Hugh. "There's a well, with a little stone chapel. See the little bucket on a rope! There's a cross on top of the chapel roof."

Cyril said, "D'you suppose this is a picture of Penrhys Mountain years ago?"

"You're right. See the valley? But there's no houses and no pit head." Hugh's depression vanished as he studied the large canvas. The colors were still bright under the film of dust which Megan wiped off carefully with the bottom of her robe.

"Yes, there's the monastery. See the monks, little tiny monks in robes like these!" They all looked down at their woolen coverings.

"To think that they were worn by holy men," said Cyril.

"Yes, they're certainly holey," said Hugh, now fully recovered, and he waggled his fingers through a big hole which threatened to split his robe into two pieces.

"We are here," and Hugh pointed to a place beneath the monastery.

The four childred clustered around the painting, their predicament forgotten in this exciting discovery.

"I wonder what the statue is doing up the tree," said Iestyn.

"Yes, you'd think it would be in the chapel or in the monastery someplace. There's one like it in the Catholic Church in Ferndale. I went there once with Rosa," said Megan.

Hugh turned away from the oil painting and put his candlestick on the mantle above the fireplace. "Wish we could light a fire," he said. "Then we could dry our wet clothes and really get warm."

"Oh, Hugh, let's! "We can tear off the panels and use the stools for firewood."

"If the chimney is blocked by stones the smoke won't get out," said Hugh. The air would be used up faster and we'd all suffocate, he thought to himself. No use in saying that to the others.

"Maybe the chimney isn't blocked," cried Megan. She pushed aside the wooden settles which sat each side of the fireplace, and crawled under the mantlepiece. Once inside she stood up. "It's big enough for Father Christmas and all his reindeer to come down," she said. "But it's dark up there."

"Could be it's night," said Cyril. "Yes, look! A star!"

"Let's see! Out of the way," yelled Iestyn.

"There's room for us all," said Hugh, noticing Cyril start to bridle.

All four stood close together looking up the chimney where a small cold light was the first sign of the outside world they had seen since they had taken refuge in the mine tunnel. Megan began to chant an old familiar rhyme. "I wish I may, I wish I might..."

"You can wish upon a star if you like, Meg Jenkins, but I know who I'm going to thank when we get home safe," interrupted Hugh.

As he contemplated climbing up the walls of the chimney, Hugh remembered the well, and he shuddered, feeling again the rush of air as he had fallen. He forced himself to ignore the jolting sensations in his body, and concentrated his attention on the present problem. The chimney wasn't as high as the well, but the walls were smoother with fewer projections to form hand and footholds.

"Maybe we can stand on each other's shoulders and hope the top one can climb out and pull the next one up. Heaviest on the bottom. Lightest on top."

Just as Hugh finished speaking, there came a rustling noise above them, and the starlight disappeared as a dark form moved across the top of the chimney.

"The ghostly monk!" whispered Megan.

They all backed away at the same time and stuck in the fire-place opening. Hugh felt panic sweep over him, and Megan and Cyril yelled at each other as each tried to be first out. Iestyn probably because he was used to waiting whenever he was in a crowd sat still and kept looking up. He pulled at Hugh's robe quietly and said, "Listen, Hugh!"

Suddenly there came a sound out of the darkness at the top of the chimney, a sound that wasn't human. Or if it was from a human, from someone insane.

"There's really something up there," said Hugh, as Megan and Cyril kneeling behind him, huddled closer, and Iestyn's small hand slid into one of his. "Listen," said Hugh urgently as the sound came again. "It reminds me of something. If it comes again I may recognize what it is."

The sound came again, unearthly, strange, yet somehow familiar. They all started yelling at the same time with instantaneous recognition. "It's a sheep," Hugh heard himself shout. Startled, the animal baaa-ed once more and moved away from the chimney top.

"Stay there and help us up," cried Iestyn.

"Yes, be a lamb," shouted Megan, and Cyril rolled about on the floor, laughing.

"Well, gang, what's our next move," asked Hugh, moving back into the underground room to consider the situation.

"Let's go out as soon as possible," said Meg. And Hugh knew she was remembering the eerie experience they had had the previous night.

"Well, I'd like to go soon, but it *is* night and we don't really know just where we are." Hugh thought longingly of the kitchen at home, with the coal fire burning cheerily and the kettle steaming on the hob. But then he thought of making their way across Penrhys Mountain with only the light of the stars to guide them.

There were pot-holes, and hollows, and sudden steep slopes, which were fun to roll down in daylight, but dangerous at night when they couldn't see where they were going.

"I hate to spend another night in this place, but I think we'd better he said with a sigh, and the picture of home faded. "We could try to light a fire, I suppose."

"Here are some old manuscripts," said Megan who went rooting into one corner of the room.

They spread the heavy parchment sheets on the floor and studied them with the candles held carefully away so that the wax did not drip on them. For Hugh realized instinctively that these must not be burned.

"It must be Latin," he said as he tried to decipher the words.

"The letters are so curly, we wouldn't know if it's Welsh, or English," said Megan. "And look at how beautiful the first letter is."

"Yes," said Hugh. "The first word of each chapter was specially colored. When Mr. Thomas took us to the museum we saw some manuscripts the monks had lettered. All done by hand."

Now that they had found an escape route, Hugh looked with more interest at the room that they were to stay in for one more night, the last one he hoped. "We've found a place that no-one has seen for years," he said.

"Maybe these manuscripts tell the story of how the statue got up the tree," said Cyril, moving across the room to look at the oil painting once more. Iestyn followed him. Megan shrieked. Hugh turned and looked up from the manuscript to where she pointed. "Iestyn's standing!"

Iestyn took his eyes from the picture and looked down at his legs. He was standing on them! Suddenly, they collapsed and Iestyn fell to the floor. Hugh moved quickly to his brother. Iestyn clung to him. "Am I healed, Hugh? Is it the waters in the well?"

"Can you stand up again?" Hugh held Iestyn, and Megan and Cyril came over to help. But Iestyn's legs gave under him. "You *were* standing!" said Hugh.

"You were looking at the picture, and forgot about your legs," Megan said. "If you did it *once* you can do it again."

"But don't try now," said Hugh quickly. He could see that Iestyn was on the verge of tears after the sudden disappointment.

"Let's rub his legs," said Cyril. And he and Megan started to massage his thin legs. Iestyn stopped crying and looked at the picture again through eyes rimmed with dust from his knuckles.

Hugh squeezed his brother's shoulder. "Don't give up," he said.

CHAPTER 15

"I'll get some coal for the fire," said Ted, as he noticed that Peg was shivering.

"It all seems like a bad dream. It was bad enough losing Dad. But he'd had a good life, and he trusted in the Lord. But to lose our three children!" Peg began to sob quietly. "We must trust in the Lord, too," said Ted. But his eyes glistened in the firelight.

"Let's light the fire!" Hugh sensed an immediate stirring of interest.

"Maybe someone will see the smoke and find us," cried Megan.

"We can dry our clothes," said Iestyn, smiling again.

"We've got to find stuff that will burn," said Hugh, "and that won't be easy."

"There's plenty of wood here," said Cyril, but when he saw Hugh's expression, he added, "I guess most of this stuff is history!"

"You're absolutely right," said Hugh. "Most of it belongs in a museum."

"Well, we're important too. We're alive and want to stay that way. The people that used these stools and things have been dead a long time. I'm sure they wouldn't mind us getting a little comfort." It was about the longest speech Cyril had made, thought Hugh. He made sense too. The memory of the hooded monk pointing the way out of that store room returned and somehow Hugh felt sure he would not mind.

And yet, those manuscripts shouldn't go up in smoke. Maybe they held important information that shouldn't be lost.

"Let's see what we can find," said Megan, and Hugh nodded approval.

"My paper bag I carried my sandwiches in." said Cyril. "I dropped it in the other room. The children scattered.

Megan found an old broom made out of twigs. Cyril returned with his brown bag and an old pallet that had served as a bed at one time. "It's leaking straw, but there's plenty left inside. It should burn well."

"I don't think I'd like to sleep on that," said Megan as she sneezed at the clouds of dust that trailed behind Cyril.

"We can always burn my crutches," said Iestyn, quietly. Hugh bit back a quick denial. Was Iestyn really healed? Or had he not really tried to walk before? But of course he had. He remembered Dad massaging his legs and holding Iestyn up while he'd tried a few steps. But he always crumpled and Dad had always caught him before he touched the floor. Maybe he had just stopped trying, and his muscles had withered from lack of use. But he had walked towards the picture, so excited that he forgot about his legs. What he had done then, he could do again. But to burn his crutches? That might be going too far. Yet, maybe, that would be a turning point for Iestyn, a kind of symbol. If so, Hugh felt he should not dissuade his brother from making this sacrifice. Besides, the crutches were replaceable, as the antique furniture was not.

Soon the children were sitting around a spitting, warming blaze. Megan and Cyril draped the wet clothes from the mantlepiece, and Iestyn stood erect, leaning on his crutches and looking into the flames. "Wish we had some of that coal we saw in the mine level," said Hugh. "The fire would burn all night then."

"Let's go back and dig some," said Cyril, laughing. "And meet the Knockers? Not me! Actually it's that cold swim I couldn't face."

Hugh thought that Cyril had changed a lot since he'd joined them. He'd never joked, just groused and grumbled all the time.

"Here goes," cried Iestyn. And one crutch landed on top of the flames, which soon licked their way around its crevices. He stood, leaning on just one crutch, his other arm against the mantlepiece. "Here's the other!" He stood for a fraction of a second without support. Then he collapsed, and Hugh grabbed him as Dad used to.

"Let me go!" yelled Iestyn fiercely. Hugh propped him up against the shelf and then let go. Iestyn held for a while, and then put his arms to his sides and collapsed on the floor. He lay there for a while and then he said, "I'm going to walk again, some time. Maybe not now. But just you wait and see!"

"Well, you helped save my life without using your legs," said Cyril.

"And you're the only one who was strong enough to push up the trapdoor," said Hugh.

"Besides digging me out," said Megan.

"I never had a brother. If I did, I'd like him to be just like you," said Cyril.

Iestyn sat up. "Thanks for cheering me up," he said, slowly.

"But nothing will ever do that if I don't get my legs back."

Hugh felt so helpless that he changed the subject, bringing out in the open thoughts he had deliberately stowed away in some dark recess of his mind.

"Does it bother any of you that by doing wrong, we were saved from being covered by the avalanche?"

Megan turned from contemplating the flames to look at Hugh. "Yes, I've thought of that. All the others who did what they were supposed to do, got buried."

"Some may have run out before the school collapsed," said Iestyn.

"Not many. It happened so fast," said Megan.

"I don't think skipping school is such a bad thing, anyway," said Cyril.

Megan laughed. "You did it often enough,"

Cyril grinned. "I'm sure glad I did that day. And that I followed you. Wow, it's been an adventure, all right."

Hugh stirred restlessly. "What's bothering me is that everyone tells you that you must be good, and then nothing bad will happen to you."

"Talk to Dad about it," said Iestyn. "He'll explain."

And Hugh remembered how his father had spent hours talking to Iestyn when he was forced to stay in bed for weeks and weeks.

"Anybody want to tell ghost stories?" he asked, suddenly feeling very light-hearted.

"I'd rather roast chestnuts," said Megan.

"Don't talk about food," said Cyril. "I can feel the fat just peeling off me." And he sucked in his cheeks and pretended his face was just skin and bone.

"You can last for years with all you've got stored up," said Megan. But her smile neutralized the insult, and Cyril laughed with her.

"We *could* torture ourselves by imagining our favorite foods," said Hugh.

"No, I couldn't stand that." Megan groaned and held her stomach. "I'm so empty I can push my hand almost through to my back."

"Insects are supposed to be full of protein," said Hugh.

"How about a stew of spiders and black pats?" There were groans all around.

"How do they live underground where there's nothing to eat?" asked Cyril. "I can see that cockroaches live in the mines because they can feed on the crumbs from the miners' lunches, but here, what can they feed on here?"

Disturbed by the fire in the fireplace a few large beetles had scuttled across into the shadowy corners. "I do hate black pats," said Megan. "They move so fast and their black shiny coats make such a crack when you step on them.

"My science books say black pats are cockroaches and they eat anything, even dirt. There's plenty of that here. And decayed plants and animals. They can survive anywhere." A long speech for Cyril. But he hadn't finished. "Besides they don't have to stay here. They can wiggle through the smallest holes and find other buildings to scrounge."

"Ugh," said Megan.

"Wish we could pin a message to 'em and send them for help," said Hugh.

"How do you know so much about insects, Cyril?" asked Megan.

"Well, I don't exactly waste time when I cut school. I've got a good butterfly collection. Would you like to see it when..." Cyril stopped suddenly and Hugh finished his sentence silently, "if we get out of here."

"Look," cried Iestyn, "there's a salamander!" He grabbed for the creature and pinioned it between his hands.

"It's like no salamander I've seen," said Hugh, leaning over to study it as it squirmed in Iestyn's grasp.

Pinkish white, about a foot long, it had three toes on its front feet and two toes each on its back feet. The skin was transparent, the color coming from the blood vessels below the surface. There didn't seem to be any eyes, probably because the lack of light made them unnecessary. On either side of its head were bright red gills.

"It looks a bit like a junior dragon," said Hugh.

"I'm going to keep him for a pet," said Iestyn.

"Watch out," said Megan. "It may grow up into a real dragon and eat us all up."

"It must live in water," said Cyril. "See those red gills? They're outside his body. That means he spends most of his time in water."

"He must live in the well," said Hugh. "Can he live out of water?"

"I'm going to keep him even if I have to crawl all the way back to the well for some water," said Iestyn.

"He'll live until we get out of here but you'll have to get a cage with his own bathroom," said Cyril, with a grin.

"How I'd love a bath," sighed Megan. "That well water was really smelly."

"All the better for algae for salamanders," said Cyril.

"You really do know your science," said Megan with admiration. "There probably were other strange wriggly creatures but it was too dark to see them."

"Well," said Hugh, "I'm going to sleep so we can get out of here as soon as it's light."

"I wonder what Dragon Mountain will look like now that most of it is in the valley," said Megan.

"Just old Penrhys Mountain like it's been since the monks lived here, and before that, I guess," said Hugh sleepily.

"Why does Wales have a dragon on its flag?" asked Iestyn.

"Go to sleep," said Hugh.

CHAPTER 16

Sleep did not come easily at the Jenkins home. When Peg closed her eyes she saw again the huge mound of mud squatting on top of the school house. She moaned and Ted reached over and held her. There was nothing he could say to comfort her or himself.

Somehow, sleep would not come. Hugh lay on one side, then the other, but the floor was cold and hard whatever position he took. He watched the smoke climb up the chimney. Soon, we'll be shimmying up too, he thought. We'll have to douse the fire if it hasn't gone out. Half asleep, he wondered how it would feel to be so light that he could rise with the smoke, the acrid smell piercing his nostrils and his relaxed body tumbling in all directions as the smoke held and carried him, pulled as by a powerful magnet, upward, and back to Pontnewydd, and Mam and Dad. He wondered if his life there would ever be the same. The school was gone. Probably many of his friends were too. How he wished morning would come so he could leave this shadowy place and breathe the clear, cold mountain-top air.

A sudden flash of white roused Hugh to wakefulness. Responding instantly he put out his hand and caught the blind creature which had run away from Iestyn straight to him. I should let it go, he thought. But Iestyn would be so disappointed. And he couldn't bear the thought of his brother's suffering even a small loss after the wrenching experience he'd had trying to walk again. It did look like a dragon. He stroked its back gently and, when its wriggling stopped, put it gently into the still damp pocket of his jacket hanging from the mantleshelf. He buttoned the pocket shut, and hoped there was enough air to keep the salamander alive. He'd like the dampness, Hugh thought.

There was only one candle left burning. All the others were just puddles of hard, grey wax. He hoped the light would last until it was time to go.

It seemed just a few moments later that Hugh woke to Megan's pushing his shoulder roughly and yelling, "It's morning!" Still befogged by sleep he thought it was Christmas morning and his sister urging him to wake and grab the bulging stocking that leaned against the brass rail at the bottom of his bed. Reality surged back into his consciousness. It was time to climb out the chimney, and go home! Megan began scrabbling at the ashes in the fireplace and howled as the last vestiges of heat injured her hand.

As she stuck her finger in her mouth, Hugh started to sing:

Mae'r bys Mary Anne wedi brifo,
  a Dafydd y gwas ddim yn iach.
Mae'r baban yn y crud yn crio.
  A'r gath wedi scrappo Johnny bach.

[Mary Anne's finger hurts,
  and David, the servant isn't well.
The baby in the crib is crying,
  and the cat has scratched little Johnny.]

While Megan stamped her foot and scowled at Hugh, the other two boys, now fully awake, sang with him:

Sospan fach yn berwi ar y tan,
  sospan fawr yn berwi ar y llawr.
A'r gath wedi scrappo Johnny bach.

[The little saucepan is boiling on the fire,
  the big saucepan is boiling on the floor.
And the cat has scratched little Johnny.]

The old nonsense rhyme that they sang on happy occasions, like when Wales won the Cup Final, rang out around the dusty panels that had heard only the silent weaving of spiders for centuries. Megan joined in when they sang the chorus a second time around, and for the third they pranced up and down the room with Iestyn beating time with his arms as he sat cross-legged in front of the fireplace. The Welsh never know when to stop when they're singing, thought Hugh. Sometimes in church at Cymanfa Ganu time, they'd sing the chorus of a favorite hymn as many as five times and just as you thought it was over, one lone, but determined voice would take up the refrain again, and everybody would sing it one more time.

"It's not just my finger but my whole hand is hurt," said Megan, but she smiled as she spoke so Hugh knew she was all right.

"Let's tackle the chimney," said Hugh. "The way I see it, we'd better form a chain, standing on each other's shoulders. We can hold on to the wall to keep our balance."

Hugh stood, his legs outspread and said, "Come on, Cyril. Then you, Meg, and then Iestyn. Let's hope Iestyn can climb out first, and reach down and pull Megan out. "I'm not sure how Cyril and I will manage, but we'll do it somehow."

"Wait, wait," cried Iestyn, "I've lost my little dragon."

Hugh remembered where he had imprisoned it, and hoped it hadn't squirmed out of his pocket and escaped. Worse even than that, what if it had died there? He quickly undid the button and out sprang the long salamander. It hung head down, its red gills quivering and its pointed snout moving from side to side, to size up the enemy it could not see with its eyeless sockets. Suddenly it darted down the jacket, so light that the coat barely moved, fell to the ground and ran across the floor directly to Iestyn sitting in front of the fireplace. "He knows me already," he cried, as he picked it up and held it against his chest, stroking its transparent back and making purring noises at it.

Hugh smiled to himself, and was glad that Iestyn was happy. "Let's go," he said. And returned to his place at the bottom of the chimney, ready to hold the human pyramid that he hoped would be tall enought to reach the outdoors.

With much jostling and strained panting, they were all in place. Hugh felt that any moment his knees would give way. He was afraid to speak or urge them to hurry for even that small expenditure of breath might be enough to disturb his balance and they would all collapse. Being the oldest is hard, he thought grimly. But then he remembered with pride his father saying, "I know I can depend on Hugh. He's my right hand man!" I can hold out a little longer he thought, though Cyril's feet bore down upon his shoulders and his toes dug sharply into his upper chest. Suddenly the heaviness slackened. "I'm up!" he heard Iestyn shout as from a long distance. Then as Cyril swayed precariously above him, he heard Megan shouting jubilantly some indistinguishable words, But Cyril's weight was still heavy.

"I can't reach your hand," Hugh heard Cyril say. Then to him, "I'm coming down, Hugh. I must be killing your shoulders."

The table, or one of the stools thought Hugh. We can stand on something and then on each other's shoulders. Of course, Megan could go for help, but Hugh hoped she would wait. He'd hate to be left down here and ignominiously pulled up by a rope. They'd come this far together. He wanted to be in at the finish. One for all, and all for one they'd said in the mine tunnel. How long ago that seemed.

"The stool isn't very sturdy, but I think the table is too wide," he said to Cyril.

"It's all the way down the passage in the first room we came to," said Cyril. "I'm game to try the stool. It may wobble a bit, but..."

Hugh leaned on it and tested it. "If we can find something to stick under this leg that's shorter." He prowled around the room and found a piece of a broken shelf that he thought would even the leg up with the others. The stool stood firm. "Wait, Hugh, let me be on the bottom this time," said Cyril. "I'm heavier than you."

"Well, in that case I'm going to carry this strip of wood from the other part of the shelf. Then you can hoist yourself up with us holding the other end." Hugh felt his head spinning with tiredness. He was glad he wouldn't have to bear Cyril on his sore shoulders. He felt Cyril sag as his full weight settled on him. He hurled up the long piece of wood, and heard Megan yelp as it almost hit her. "You should have been watching," he yelled in exasperation. "Where are you?"

Two grimy faces appeared at the top of the chimney opening.

"Sorry, Hugh, but wait till you see what we've seen!" Megan sounded ecstatic. Hugh bit back another angry retort. "Get me up," he said tersely.

"It's a bit narrow at the top," said Megan. "It may be hard for you to squeeze through." Now she tells me, he thought.

"Get Iestyn to hang on to your legs and try to reach me with your hand," he said. He had thought this part was going to be easy. What if he stuck in the hole? He felt Cyril wince as he stretched up to his full height with one hand on the wall and the other straining to touch Megan's fingers. There! His fingers crawled up her hand to her wrist and then clung there tight as a vise. Slowly, hearing much scuffling above his head, Hugh felt himself being pulled up. Megan let go his hand and grabbed his shoulders, and for the first time in days Hugh saw green grass and blue sky. Iestyn got his arms around Hugh's chest and like a cork popping out of a bottle Hugh emerged from the chimney and collapsed on the grass.

However can we get Cyril through that opening? Hugh felt weariness and despair sweep over him. This was just too much.

"Hugh, look!" shouted Megan. "A lamb, we saw it born."

"We saw the head first, so we're going to be pushed ahead," cried Iestyn, still stroking his white salamander.

Hugh watched as the white woolly lamb tugged at its mother hungrily. Its long tail twitched, and Megan said, "You're lucky, because you saw the tail first." In spite of his irritation at his sister's preoccupation with the lamb, rather than the problem of getting Cyril out of the underground room, Hugh felt the tenseness seep out of him. The contrast of the dead dust of the buried monastery with the life around him, the scudding clouds, the dewy brightness of the grass, the eager nuzzling of the new-born lamb, even the placid browsing of the ewe, made him suddenly want to shout for joy. And he did, jumping in the air, frightening the mother sheep so that she scurried away, her bleating offspring at her side, trying to suck and run at the same time.

"Oh, Hugh, look what you've done," cried Megan. But when they saw the lamb resume its feeding in a far corner of the field, she too joined Hugh in a noisy celebration of their return to the open air.

Iestyn gave his full attention to the salamander, which wriggled and struggled to get out of his grasp. "Poor thing," said Hugh. "The light probably hurts it, though it doesn't have eyes."

"Maybe you should let it go back to the darkness," said Megan.

"No, I'll keep it in a box in the cwtch under the stairs. It'll be dark enough there."

"Mam might have something to say about that," said Megan, and Hugh nudged her to stop. Why worry Iestyn now?

"She won't complain if he eats the black pats," said Megan, responding to Hugh's signal. "What are you going to call him, Iestyn?"

"Cymro," said Iestyn. "He's like the red dragon on the flag."

A forlorn shout reminded them that Cyril was still below. Hugh lay on his stomach and peered down. All he could see was Cyril's white face looking hopefully upward.

"Can you pile two stools on top of each other, and reach this piece of shelf?" He waited and listened. Suddenly he knew the stools had toppled over. Cyril yelled "Uffern!" And Hugh didn't blame him. It was an awful place down there, not as bad as burning fire, of course, but its dusty silence had been almost as suffocating as death itself. And he'd had company down there. Cyril was alone, with the fear of abandonment his only company. He looked around the field and saw a gate. This must be a sheep fold where the farmer put ewes when they were ready for lambing. Many of course ranged free over the mountain pasture and had their lambs in the open. Stubborn things, sheep, but after his recent experience of being penned up, Hugh didn't blame the ones that got away, though they led the farmer a merry chase when he tried to catch them and their offspring for inoculation. As he walked over to the gate he saw that the wooden latch hung broken and the gate was secured by a rope. Hugh couldn't believe his eyes. What luck! The rope was thick but rather frayed. I hope it will hold Cyril, Hugh thought. Then he ran back to the hole where Megan and Iestyn were calling down to Cyril to reassure him that they hadn't left.

"It's not as long as I'd like," he said. Hugh wished he could tie one end to a tree or something but it wouldn't stretch that far.

"Iestyn, you're the strongest. You be the anchor. It'll have to be tug-o-war, with everyone a winner if Cyril gets up safely. But wait!" Hugh suddenly remembered what a tight squeeze he'd had, and Cyril was pudgier. He sat back on his heels and reviewed the situation.

In the back of his mind had been the question, why hadn't the buried rooms been discovered long before this? He noted that there were large rocks around the aperture, possibly from the walls of the monastery which had stood on this site. They had probably covered the chimney so that the farmers that had owned the land successfully for centuries had not realized what lay beneath their sheep-grazing ground. What had moved the heavy rocks? Looking down to the valley below, Hugh could see the wide swathe the avalance had torn out of the hillside. Of course! The force of the avalanche! Hugh remembered with a shudder the earth shaking, the convulsions that had woken Dragon Mountain out of its centuries-old slumber to become a force that destroyed the school-house and its occupants. That must be it. He started lifting rocks away from the opening to make more room for Cyril to climb through. Some were too heavy to shift without a crowbar but there were smaller ones that he could remove. Even an inch or two would make a difference.

"Say, Cyril," he hollered down the chimney. "Bring as many of those manuscripts as you can carry." And he heard Cyril run over to the corner where they had discovered them. When he returned, Hugh threw down the rope. It wasn't long enough! Hugh could see Cyril's eyes widen in frustration. "Stand on a stool!" Hugh shouted and soon saw Cyril grab the end of the rope. "Brace yourself against the wall with your feet," cried Hugh. "It will take some of the weight off us." Hugh dug his feet into the turf and he felt Megan bracing herself. He couldn't see Iestyn but he knew his strong wrists would not give way easily. Slowly, Cyril's head came closer and higher, and just when Hugh felt his arms would pull out of their sockets, Cyril's upper body appeared. Letting go of the rope, Cyril leaned on the ground as Hugh had done, and stayed there panting, his hips and legs still held in the hole. Cyril grinned, and breathed deeply. "Well! Half of me's out!" he said. He seemed content just to stay that way for a while. "This'll teach me to lose weight," he said. "You skinny ones have all the luck! Here, take these manuscripts."

The others tugged at more stones to widen the hole, and Cyril squirmed and twisted until he too was free. His legs were scratched and bloody, but he was all in one piece. Hugh clapped him on the shoulder, and Cyril muttered a brusque thanks in Welsh, "Diolch yn fawr!" while Iestyn shouted a "Yo, Cyril!"

Before the children started their walk back to home and family, Hugh reminded them that they should cover up the chimney but be sure to mark the place so they could find it again. "I think we've made a discovery that is very important. We don't want it spoiled before experts in history can see it. Besides some one could fall down that hole. Even a sheep could break a leg." So all four children moved the stones back so that the chimney was concealed. "Must put the rope back on the gate, after we're through." And the tired trio still managed to wrest enough energy from their muscles and spirits to manage a cheer and a skipping step or two as they moved towards the gate and freedom.

"Ta, ta, little lamb," cried Megan. And Iestyn murmured loving words to Cymro, the salamander.

CHAPTER 17

The slag had all been removed. Piles of stone, and slate, and brick were spread all over the schoolyard as though a giant had been playing with building blocks and had discarded them carelessly. There were no people there. The village had given up the search.

Hugh looked back. Iestyn was still sitting on the grass. "I'll wait here until you send someone to get me," he said.

Hugh realized that his brother was much too tired to drag himself along. His hands were red and swollen, and what he could see of his knees through his torn trouser looked scarred and scratched. He had been so plucky all the way. Hugh hesitated to suggest carrying him on his back because he knew how independent Iestyn was. Cyril broke into his thoughts, "All for one, and one for all, remember? No one gets left behind. Make a seat with me, Hugh."

Iestyn hesitated. "You and Hugh saved my life. I want to carry you home like the champion you are." Cyril's voice was matter-of-fact and brooked no refusal. Megan helped Iestyn climb on the boys' clasped arms, lowered as close to the ground as they could get.

Megan led the way, opening the gate and then tying it shut with the rope they'd used to pull up Cyril. Hugh saw her look over to the baby lamb. She wouldn't want it to leave the safety of the sheepfold. "We'd better take the road, not the steep path," he said.

When they reached the steps, Iestyn suggested he sit on the rail that helped people climb up. "I've always wanted to slide down the bannisters," he said. They had no curved staircase and bannister in their small house. Just a narrow enclosed stairway. Hugh and Cyril stood on each side of him, to make sure he didn't fall off. Hugh felt different arm muscles complain as they kept Iestyn from sliding too fast.

They could hear singing as they approached the chapel at the foot of the hill. "Is it Sunday, then?" asked Megan. "I've lost count of the days." Even though it was March Hugh could see the big front doors standing wide open, and there were people standing in the vestibule. "Looks like a full house," he said. "Let's hope we can go by without them seeing us."

"We aren't exactly looking our Sunday best," said Megan.

Suddenly, there were pointing fingers, and some of the people in the vestibule moved to the front steps. The organ and the singing stopped. The children stood as though transfixed while the congregation poured out of all the doors and crossed the street towards them.

Then Hugh could see his father and mother, pushing through the crowd. His mother got to them first, and somehow all four of them were enfolded by her arms. His father hugged them from behind and Hugh felt for the first time in days that he was safe in a circle of love. He didn't have to plan anymore, to be brave anymore. He could relax and just be!

Mr. Williams, the Minister, his black robe billowing behind him, ran across the lawn to them. Suddenly, Dai Jones, him with the deep bass voice, started to sing: "Praise God from whom all blessings flow." Everyone joined in, and not even the Morlais Choir at the Eisteddfod sounded so glorious to Hugh. He tried to sing too, but his throat tightened and he had to fight back the tears of joy that filled his eyes.

Reverend Williams put his hand on each of their heads. "Thank you, Lord. Diolch yn fawr." He seemed too moved to say more. "Better get them home, Peg," he said.

Dad lifted Iestyn on his shoulders. “No talking now. Home it is.” He put his arm around Hugh, and Hugh could see that Mam and Megan were so close it looked as though they never could be separated again.

“Cyril!” Glyn’s voice rang out over the singing. They started towards each other and Hugh smiled to see Cyril’s face as his father grabbed him in a bear hug.

Homeward they went, the crowd behind them, singing all the way. “It’s like being in the Cardiff opera,” said Megan, pulling on Iestyn’s trouser leg.

“Soccer champions, more like,” said Iestyn.

When the Jenkins arrived at their warm kitchen, Mam said, “Food, first. Bed next. Talk later.”

“Just one thing, Mam,” said Hugh. “It’s so good to be home!”

But before they went to bed they sat together in front of the fireplace. Hugh sighed in contentment. Then he remembered that some children would not be with their families, ever again. “What about the others?” he asked.

His father stirred the pieces of coal into active flame before replying. “They are with God,” he said quietly.

“But why...?” Hugh persisted.

“Life and death are mysteries. Maybe we are wrong to think of death as an end. Maybe it’s the beginning of something better.”

Hugh told them about Grampa and the monk who showed them where the trapdoor was.

Peg Jenkins smiled though her cheeks glistened in the firelight. “When I prayed for all the children, and most of all for you three, I seemed to hear a voice within me saying, ‘He gathered them in His arms.’ And even though the sadness didn’t go away, I felt comforted.”

"But why were we saved, when we were wrong to skip school?" Hugh asked.

"Thank God you did," said Father. "You know God doesn't only love us when we're good. And I don't believe He caused that terrible mud slide. Men piled up all that slag and small coal because it cost too much to cart it away."

Iestyn stirred in his chair and half-opened his eyes. "Do miracles still happen?" he asked.

"Of course," said Mother. "You're home, safe and sound. That's enough miracle for me!" Then she screamed, "What's that?" as the white salamander with the red gills climbed out of Iestyn's pocket.

"That's Cymro, Iestyn's little dragon," said Megan. He brought us luck, and so we rescued him too."

"Well, I don't want him running around. You'll have to find a cage for him."

"I'll keep him in the cwtch and maybe he'll eat all the black pats," said Iestyn. He yawned and then asked, "Why does the Welsh flag have a red dragon on it? Hugh wouldn't tell me."

"Well, you ask too many questions. Besides, I didn't know the answer," snapped Hugh. His mother and father exchanged looks which Hugh guessed meant that they thought things were back to normal.

"Is it because of the coal?" asked Megan. "The dragon breathes out fire that keeps us warm."

"There's clever you are, fy nghariadi," said Father. "But I don't think that's the reason. The Welsh needed to be fierce like the dragon to keep invaders out of the country. And the true fire of the Welsh comes from warm hearts, a love of song, and most of all from faith in God. Now that is the best fire of all."

Hugh sank gratefully into the warm spot in his bed where the paper-wrapped brick, hot from the oven had been. He stretched his feet slowly until he found it at the bottom of the bed. It was still too hot to rest his feet on it but it was good to feel its heat taking the chill off the cold sheets. He remembered the morning the adventure had begun, and without bothering to put on his slippers tip-toed past Iestyn who was already asleep and went into Megan's room where he could look up at the mountain. The tip had gone. The green hills still undulated around the village but all resemblance to a dragon had gone too. It was Penrhys Mountain again. Hugh yawned and went back to bed.

GLOSSARY

Bore da	Good morning
butties	partners or pals
coblynau	supernatural little men in mythical tales that help miners find coal
cwtch	closet of alcove under the stairs or a place to store coal
diolch yn fawr	Thank (you) very much
Duw	God
eisteddfod	a festival in which people compete for prizes in music, poetry and recitation (literally a sit-down!)
faggots	meat cakes similar to hamburgers made from minced or chopped liver
fy nghariadi	my dear one, or my love
Jawch	an expletive
lorry	truck or van
Mabinogion	a collection of tales from the mythic history of the Welsh

mitching	playing truant, skipping school
trews	trousers
tylwyth teg	the wee folk; fairies
Uffern	an expletive: hell
whipperin	truant officer: probably from “whip her in”
Gymanfa Ganu	a gathering for hymn singing

www.ingramcontent.com/pod-product-compliance
Ingram Content Group UK Ltd.
Pitfield, Milton Keynes, MK11 3LW, UK
UKHW041934190726
13854UKWH00004B/1576